A Corner of the Universe

A Corner
of the Universe

Ann M. Martin

SCHOLASTIC INC.

New York Toronto London Auckland Sydney
Mexico City New Delhi Hong Kong Buenos Aires

ISBN 0-439-57923-6

12 11 10 9 8 7 6 5 4   3 4 5 6 7 8/0

Printed in the U.S.A.   23

First Scholastic Book Club printing, September 2003

Book design by Elizabeth B. Parisi

In memory of
Stephen Dole Matthews
June 6, 1927 – August 14, 1950

This book is for my friend,
Jean Feiwel,
who knows how to lift the corners.

Last summer, the summer I turned twelve, was the summer Adam came. And forever after I will think of events as Before Adam or After Adam. Tonight, which is several months After Adam, I finally have an evening alone.

I am sitting in our parlor, inspecting our home movies, which are lined up in a metal box. Each reel of film is carefully labeled. WEDDING DAY — 1945. VISIT WITH HAYDEN — 1947. HATTIE — 1951. FOURTH OF JULY — 1958. I look for the films from this summer. Dad has spliced them together onto a big reel labeled JUNE–JULY 1960. I hold it in my hands, turn it over and over.

The evening is quiet. I feel like I am the only one at home, even though two of the rooms upstairs are occupied. I hear the clocks in Mr. Penny's room, and footsteps padding down the hall to the bathroom. The footsteps belong to Miss Hagerty, I'm sure of it. I know the routines of our boarders, and now is the hour when Miss Hagerty, who is past eighty, begins what she calls her nightly beauty regime. Outside, a car glides down Grant Avenue, sending its headlights circling around the darkened living room. It's warm for October, and so I have cracked one window open. I can smell leaves, hear a dog barking.

Mom and Dad have gone with Nana and Papa to some big dinner at the Present Day Club, their first true social event since Nana and Papa's party on that awful night in July. On this first night to myself, Dad has entrusted me with his movie projector and all the reels of film. I made popcorn and am eating it in the parlor where technically I am not supposed to eat anything, following the unfortunate deviled egg incident of 1958. Really, you can only see the edges of the stain, plus I'm twelve now, not some little ten-year-old. I would think the food ban could be lifted, since Dad feels that I am responsible enough to operate his movie equipment.

He said I could do everything myself this evening, and I have, without a single mistake or accident. I set up the screen at one end of the parlor. I lugged the projector out of the closet, hoisted it onto a table, and threaded it with a reel of film, making all the right loops. Turned on the projector, turned off the light, put the bowl of popcorn on a pot holder in my lap, and settled in to watch the film labeled HATTIE — 1951. It's one of my favorites because my third birthday party is on it and I can watch our old cat Simon jump up on the dining room table and land in a dish of ice cream. Then I can play the film backward and watch Simon fly down to the floor and see all the splashes of ice cream slurp themselves back into the dish. I made Simon jump in and out several times before I watched the rest of the film.

But now I am holding the tin from this summer. I consider it for a long time before I take out the reel and fasten it to the side of the projector. I thread and loop and wind, doing everything by the light of a little reading lamp. When I finish, my hands are shaking. I draw in a deep breath, turn on the projector, turn off the light, sit back.

Well. There is Angel Valentine, the very first thing. She is standing on our front porch, waving at the camera. We have an awful lot of shots of people standing on our front porch, waving at the camera. That's because when Dad pulls out his camera and starts aiming it around, someone is bound to say, "Oh, Lord, not the movie camera. I don't know what to do!" And Dad always replies, "Well, how about if you just stand on the porch and wave?" So there is Angel waving. Pretty soon Miss Hagerty and Mr. Penny step out of the house and stand one on each side of Angel and they wave too.

And then later, on another day, in dimmer light, I see Nana and Papa standing on their own front porch, waving.

They are dressed for a party. Papa is in his tux with shiny shoes, and Nana is wearing a long dress, all the way to her ankles, a shawl wrapped around her shoulders. I don't remember where they were going, dressed like that. But they are happy, smiling, their arms linked, Papa patting Nana's hand.

And then suddenly there is Adam. He won't smile or wave at the camera. He would never do anything you asked him to do when the movie camera was out. So he is standing in our yard tossing a baseball up and down, up and down. When the front door opens and Angel steps out, looking fresh and cool in a sleeveless summer dress, he drops the ball at his feet and stares at her as she waves at Dad, then sits on the porch swing and opens a book. I play the scene backward, then watch it again. Not for the entertainment value, but so I can see Adam once more.

Next comes the carnival. I sit up straighter. There's the Ferris wheel. Mom and I are riding it around and around, feeling awkward because Dad won't turn off the camera. We smile and smile and smile some more, huge smiles that eventually begin to look branded onto our faces. And there's the Fourth of July band concert, our picnic spread in front of us. Adam is eating in a machine-like way, refusing to look at the camera. Everyone else dutifully makes yummy motions, pats their stomachs, grins in Dad's direction. I let out a quiet burp, for Adam's benefit, which makes him laugh.

Finally there is my birthday party — the one Mom and Dad gave, not Adam's. Adam's was private. And it was a once-in-a-lifetime event. This party is the one we have every year. I look at the cake, the presents. No Simon now. He died when I was five, and we never got another pet. Everyone is laughing — Mom, Nana, Papa, Cookie, Miss Hagerty, Mr. Penny, Angel, me. Everyone except Adam, who is focused on the decorations on my cake. We don't know it yet, but this is the beginning of the sugar rose incident, and Adam is about to storm off and Dad is about to stop filming.

Presently the reel clicks to an end and the tail of the film flaps around. I turn the projector off and sit in the dark for a few moments, thinking about all those happy images. The smiling, the waving. I want to cry. My father's movies are great, but they don't begin to tell the story of the summer. What's left out is more important than what is there. Dad captured the good times, only the good times.

The parts he left out are what changed my life.

One

On early summer mornings, Millerton is a sleepy town, the houses nodding in the heavy air. Not even six-thirty and I can feel the humidity seeping through the window shades and covering me like a blanket. Everything I touch is damp.

I'm pretty sure I am the only one in the house who is awake. I lie in bed for a while, listening to the birds. I'm not about to spend the morning in bed, though, even if it is the first day of summer vacation. Some of my classmates wait all year long for summer just so they can sleep late every morning. Not me. I have way too much to do. I roll out of bed, dress in shorts and sandals and the sleeveless blouse Miss Hagerty made for me on her Singer sewing machine. The blouse is white with a big X of blue rickrack across the front.

I tiptoe down the hallway. My room is at one end, the

staircase at the other. In between are my parents' room, Miss Hagerty's room, Mr. Penny's room, Angel Valentine's room, a small guest room, a bathroom, a powder room. (It is a long hallway.) It must be 6:45, because just as I pass Mr. Penny's room, it erupts with chiming and clanging and peeping and chirping. Mr. Penny used to run a clock repair shop. He's retired now, but his room is filled with clocks, and of course they all run perfectly. At quarter past, half past, and quarter to every hour, they ding and cheep and whir, sounds we have all grown used to and can sleep through at night. On the hour itself, cuckoos pop out of their wooden houses, one clock chimes like a ship's bell, animals waltz, skaters glide. Mr. Penny even has a grandfather clock, which I think he should have, since he could be a grandfather if he had ever had any children. A sun and a moon move across the face of that clock. And even though Mr. Penny is not one for kids (not now, never has been), he lets me wind it with the little crank once a week, keeping my eye on the weights inside until they are in just the right position. Mr. Penny says I am responsible.

I tiptoe down the stairs and into the kitchen. I am still the only one up. This is good. If I'm going to start breakfast for everyone I like to have the kitchen to myself. I set out some of the things Cookie will need when she arrives. Cookie is our cook and she helps Mom with the meals for our boarders. Her real name is Raye Bennett, which I think is beautiful, a name for a heroine in a novel, but everyone calls her Cookie, so I do too. I sometimes wonder if she wouldn't like to be called Raye or Mrs. Bennett, but nobody in our family asks too many questions.

In the summer I am in charge of Miss Hagerty's breakfast tray. Miss Hagerty is the only one of our boarders who takes breakfast in her room. This is primarily because she is old, but also because oh my goodness no one must see her before she has had a chance to put her face on, and she needs energy for that job. So every morning I make up her tray, which is always the same — a soft-boiled egg in a cup, a plate of toast with the crusts cut off, and a pot of tea. Since Miss Hagerty appreciates beauty, I put a pansy in a bud vase in the corner of her tray.

Seven-fifteen now, a key in the front door, and suddenly the kitchen comes alive. Cookie bustles in at the same time Mom and Dad stumble downstairs. My parents are still in their pajamas, smelling of sleep, and in Dad's case, of Lavoris mouthwash.

"Good morning," I say.

"Good morning!" cries Cookie, always cheerful.

"Morning," mumble Mom and Dad.

Mom collapses onto a kitchen chair. "Hattie," she says, "you've already fixed Miss Hagerty's tray?"

Well, yes. I am holding it right in front of me.

"She's industrious," says Cookie, who has opened four cupboards, taken the carton of eggs out of the refrigerator, and turned on the fire under the skillet. "Like me."

I am pleased by Cookie's comment, but I don't know what to say, so I say nothing.

Mom considers me. "She could be a little less industrious and a little more outgoing."

I stalk out of the kitchen, the moment ruined. I would like to stomp up the stairs, but I can't since I am carrying the tray and I don't want to slosh tea around.

I knock at Miss Hagerty's door.

"Dearie?" she calls. For as long as I have known Miss Hagerty (which is all my life, because she has lived in our boardinghouse since before I was born), she has never called me anything but Dearie. When I was little, I thought maybe she couldn't remember my name. But I notice she doesn't call anyone else Dearie, so I am pleased that it is her special name for me.

"Morning, Miss Hagerty," I call back. "Can I come in?"

"*Entrez,*" she replies grandly.

I balance the tray on one hand and open the door with my other. I am just about the only person who is allowed to see Miss Hagerty early in the morning before she has put her face on. And she is something. She is propped up in bed, a great perfumy mountain. Some of the mountain is Miss Hagerty's astonishing bedding — floral sheets and quilts and lace-edged pillows, woolen throws that Miss Hagerty and her friends knitted. She sleeps under the same mound of bedding whether the temperature is 90 degrees or 20 degrees. The rest of the mountain is Miss Hagerty herself. Miss Hagerty reminds me of her bedding — soft and perfumed, her plump body always draped in floral.

I place the tray on Miss Hagerty's lap. She prefers to eat her breakfast in bed. I draw back her curtains, then sit in an armchair and look around. There is barely a free inch of space in Miss Hagerty's room. The sewing table is piled high with fabric. From her quilted sewing bags spill cards of lace and bias tape, buttons and needles and snaps. Every other surface of the room is covered with perfume bottles, china birds, wooden boxes, and glass bud vases.

Neatly arranged on her dresser are twelve framed photos of me, one taken on the day I was born, and the others taken on each of my birthdays since then. I see myself change from a chubby baby to a chubby toddler to a skinny little girl to a skinny older girl, watch my hair lighten to near white, see the curls fall away to be replaced by braids. I think the photo mirror is a great honor. Miss Hagerty says she considers me her granddaughter. And I wish she were my grandmother. That has to be a private wish, though, since I already have two grandmothers. It's just that Granny lives in Kentucky and I hardly ever see her, and Nana . . . well, Nana is Nana.

"Miss Hagerty," I say while she begins the process of

slathering the toast with the egg, which she has mushed up in its cup, "what's wrong with being shy?"

"Nothing at all, Dearie. Why?"

"I don't know." I can't quite look at Miss Hagerty.

"Well, don't you worry about getting a boyfriend. Trust me, even shy girls get boyfriends."

That was the last thing on my mind, but it is a fascinating thought. Almost as fascinating as the fact that Miss Hagerty, never married herself, is practically an expert on boyfriends and husbands. Not to mention on hairstyling and makeup. She is always saying things to me like, "Dearie, you could soften those sharp cheekbones of yours with a little blush — right here." Or, "Look, Dearie, how this eyeliner will make your gray eyes spring to life." I am not allowed to wear makeup yet, but I store up these tips for when I am in high school.

Later, when I leave Miss Hagerty's room with the breakfast tray, I try to imagine myself with a boyfriend. I could be like Zelda Gilroy on *Dobie Gillis*. Or maybe I should be like Thalia Menninger, since she's the girl Dobie is always after. And I wouldn't put him off, like Thalia does. I would be happy to sit with Dobie in the malt shop. He's a little old for me, but he's awfully cute. I would wear swirly skirts, and blouses with puffy sleeves, and wide patent leather belts, and I would tease my hair so it puffed out behind a pink elastic headband. At the malt shop, Dobie and I would buy one malt with two straws so we could sip from it together, and everyone who saw us would know we were boyfriend and girlfriend. I only hope that Dobie would do the talking for both of us and it really wouldn't matter that I'm shy.

As I carry Miss Hagerty's tray down the hall Mr. Penny comes out of his room wearing wrinkled pants and a wrinkled shirt, and his morning face. I say, "Hi, Mr. Penny," and keep on going because he absolutely cannot have a conversation until he has a cup of coffee in him.

I take the tray back to the kitchen, and join Mom and Dad, now dressed and fresh looking, in the dining room for breakfast. Mr. Penny will join us later, I know, but Angel Valentine will not. Angel watches her waistline, plus she is ambitious about her secretarial job at the bank, and she says it makes a good impression if she is at her desk in the morning before her boss arrives. So Angel breezes into the dining room dressed like one of those Dobie Gillis girls, gulps down a cup of coffee, and runs out the door calling, "Enjoy your first day of vacation, Hattie."

I think Angel is absolutely wonderful, and I wish I were her little sister, even though I have known her for only a month.

After breakfast, everybody bustles off. Mr. Penny, who is

generally in a hurry, says he must go into town lickety-split, right now, he has errands to do. Miss Hagerty decides to sit on the front porch and knit. Cookie gets busy with lunch. Toby diAngeli shows up to help Mom clean the bedrooms. And Dad goes to work in his third-floor studio.

My father is an artist. He has been commissioned to paint two portraits for a friend of Nana and Papa's. I plan to stand behind him and watch, which Dad swears does not make him nervous. Mostly what I watch are his right hand and the paintbrush at the end of it. That hand, the one that's so important to him that he has actually tried to insure it, is a wondrous thing. Stained with ink, sticky with paint, fingernails surrounded by grime that can only be removed with turpentine, his hand flashes a paintbrush across a canvas and transforms it from a wash of white to a face or a country road or a bowl of fruit, with depth and light and shadows. I feel like I am watching a magician.

Sometimes Dad gives me a small canvas of my own and we paint together. I stick to abstracts, except for horses.

My father is almost always doing something interesting. If he's not painting, then he's working in our gardens. Or fixing something in the house. Or making greeting cards (he can even make the kind that pop up). Or taking photos and developing them himself. Or running around with the movie camera. Which is why I can feel that angry flush creep across my cheeks whenever Nana implies that Mom married beneath her. My father can do anything, it seems. But according to Nana he has cast a shadow on our family by turning our home into a boardinghouse. Dad, however, says he is lucky to be able to support his family and his career by running the boardinghouse.

I hurry up the stairs to the third floor and am about to dash into Dad's studio when I come to such a fast stop that I have to grab on to the door to catch myself. I have almost stepped on Dad's project.

He's not painting after all.

"Ooh, what is this?" I say. "Another movie?" Dad spent several weeks last year making an animated movie called *Queen for a Day.* In it a very mean cardboard queen with curly hair chases her husband the king all around their castle, trying to kill him. The king gets the better of her, though, and has her head chopped off. At which point, the queen flies up to heaven with angel wings but is turned away and sent downward to be consumed by orange and red paper flames. The movie is three and a half minutes long. I have watched it over and over again. I am about the only audience the movie has ever had.

I look at what is spread on the floor now. I do not see any queens or flames or angel wings. What I see instead are hundreds of pieces of paper in varying sizes, shapes, and colors. As I watch, my father inches a small blue paper circle closer to a larger blue paper circle. Then he takes a frame of it with his 16-millimeter movie camera.

"It's called *Abstract*," Dad replies. "The shapes are going to move all around the screen. They'll rearrange themselves, form new patterns. The colors will shift. . . ." He inches the circle even closer to the other circle, then edges a tiny blue dot into the picture.

I think about Nana. Nana wishes Dad had a real job, like Papa does. She wishes he were a lawyer or a businessman, something proper. But an artist? Worse, an artist who sometimes makes things he's not even going to sell?

As if Dad is reading my mind, he says, still inching those shapes around, "By the way, Nana is coming over for lunch today."

"Nana?" I repeat.

"Yes."

"Is coming for lunch?"

"Yes."

"Coming over here for lunch?"

"Yes."

"For lunch today?"

Dad looks up and smiles at me. "We'll survive, Hattie."

I am not so sure. Suddenly I feel like getting out of the house. I look at my watch. Ten o'clock. That is a fine time for my daily walk into town. Plus on the way I have to stop at Betsy's to say good-bye to her. If I take long enough with both of these activities maybe I'll miss lunch altogether.

"I'm going over to Betsy's," I say. "See you later."

I don't know whether Dad hears me. He has to fiddle with that dot.

Two

There are only three rules at the boardinghouse (if you don't count the food-in-the-parlor ban): 1. Every boarder must pay rent on the first of the month, even if the first falls on a Sunday. 2. No pets (this rule was put into effect the day after Simon died). 3. Visitors of the opposite sex may be entertained only on the front porch or in the parlor. Mom says all these rules apply to me as well, including number one if I decide to live at home beyond the age of eighteen. I'm not sure if she's kidding about this.

Since there is no rule about telling Mom and Dad where I'm going, I often leave without saying anything — but not so often that they might decide to create a rule about it. The thing is, Millerton is a very small town, everybody knows everybody, and everybody likes to gossip. Half the time when I get back from one of my walks into town, Mom already knows where I've been. Mrs. Evans down the street will have called to say, "I just saw Hattie go by," and then Mr. Shucard, who runs the Meat Wagon, will have called to say, "Hattie's on her way to the library again," and an hour later Mrs. Moore, the librarian, will have called to say, "Hattie just checked out ten more books, Dorothy." So there's hardly any need for me to say where I'm going all the time.

I rush through the second-floor hall, hoping to avoid Mom and Toby, who have both vacuum cleaners up and running and might try to hand one of them to me. Toby has to come over three times every week in order for us to keep the boardinghouse clean.

Our house is an enigma, which is a word from one of my sixth-grade vocabulary lists. It is the third largest house in all of Millerton, but nobody considers it a mansion, which is what everybody considers Nana and Papa's house, the second largest in town. Our house was a ramshackle mess when Mom and Dad bought it just after they got married. I have seen it in a movie that Dad took in 1946, and it looks like a house from a scary Halloween story. The paint was peeling off, the shutters were hanging at angles, entire steps were missing from the staircase, windows were broken. It had been slated for demolition — until Mom and Dad bought it with the money Nana and Papa gave them for their wedding. Bought it for a song, as Dad is fond of saying. Mom and Dad and their friends set to work fixing it up and turning it into the boardinghouse, and Miss Hagerty was able to move in before I was born.

Now it's a very nice house, but it does not compare with Nana and Papa's grand one. Our house (according to Nana) is a business, and theirs is a home. At our house, Mom helps Cookie with the cooking and Toby with the cleaning, Dad tends the gardens, and when we need to go somewhere we hop in our ancient Ford station wagon and Dad drives. At Nana and Papa's, the cooks cook, the maids clean, the gardeners garden, and the chauffeur drives. And he does not drive a used Ford station wagon, which, by the way, Nana and Papa offered to replace three years ago with a nice new station wagon, but Dad put his foot down and privately told Mom that we are not a charity case.

Our house looks like one thing, but it is something else altogether.

Five seconds later I am down the stairs and have shot through the front door and called good-bye to Miss Hagerty, whose needles are clacking away, a long heathery shawl trailing off of them and piling up in her lap. I run across our lawn to the sidewalk, then down Grant Avenue two blocks to Betsy's house. As I suspected, the McGruder family Ford station wagon (just like ours, only brand-new) is parked in the driveway, every door open. The car is pretty much jam-packed and still one McGruder after another comes bustling out of the house carrying something else to be added to the load. I think of the *I Love Lucy* episode in which Fred Mertz packs the Ricardos' car for their trip to California, tying boxes and suitcases in precarious piles everywhere, including on the hood. The inside of the McGruders' car is packed to the very roof, except for a tunnel through which Mr. McGruder can peer when he looks in the rearview mirror. Mrs. McGruder and Randy, Betsy's older brother, are busily tying things to the roof rack on top of the car. And there is still stuff on the lawn waiting to be added to the load.

Every year it is the same. The day after school ends, Betsy's family takes off for two entire months at their house in Maine. I always think they will never get the car packed, but then they do, and they leave, and I don't see Betsy again until shortly before school starts. Betsy is my best friend (technically, she is my only friend), and we have never once spent summer vacation together.

Betsy struggles through the McGruders' front door carrying two more suitcases, sees me standing on the sidewalk, drops the suitcases, and waves.

"Hi!" she calls. "I didn't know if you were coming."

Well. I have come to see Betsy off every year of our lives since we were five.

"I brought you something," I say, pulling three pieces of Bazooka bubble gum out of the pocket of my shorts. "Save the comics," I add.

"And I'll send away for the free stuff," says Betsy. She pauses. "I wish you would come with us."

I look at my feet, the ground. "I know. I'm sorry."

For the past three years the McGruders have invited me to spend the summer with them, and each time I have thanked them and thanked them, then said no. Mom cannot get over this. A free trip to Maine. Two months of swimming and lobsters and hiking and fir trees. It sounds wonderful, but I don't want to go. I also don't want to go when Nana offers (as she has for the past four years) to send me to overnight camp in Vermont, the very same camp Mom went to when she was my age. These trips sound nice, but I just want to spend the summer in Millerton — visiting with Miss Hagerty, painting with Dad, walking downtown, and reading my piles of library books. Besides, what if I were to get sick while I was away? I have never been away from home without my parents, and I am not about to start now. Mom says, "What are you going to do when it's time to go to college?" I choose not to think about that yet. That is years away. For now, I just want things all safe and familiar. My life may not be perfect, but it is what I have known.

Miraculously, the McGruders manage to pack their car in

a manner suggesting that it will not tip over before they reach Southwest Harbor. Betsy and I hug, promise to write every day, and then wave to each other until the station wagon is out of sight.

I continue downtown. I take this same walk nearly every day in the summer. I don't always go at the same time, but I always take the same route. A block after Betsy's house, I turn left onto Nassau Street, and walk along it, passing by some of Millerton's finer houses. They are not as large as ours, but they are as grand as Nana and Papa's. My favorite features a fountain smack in the center of the front yard, an enormous daffodil showering the marble beneath it day and night.

The grand houses give way to a few smaller houses, and suddenly I am in downtown Millerton. I let out a little sigh. I love Millerton. I hope I never have to leave it.

I always walk along the east side of Nassau Street first. I check out the Garden Theater to see what's playing there. Lately, Mr. and Mrs. Finch, who run the theater, have been holding a Shirley Temple Festival, which does not really interest me. Sure enough, the marquee reads *Baby Take a Bow.* Oh, well, I'll just have to wait for something new. I don't have a spare quarter anyway. Nana would probably treat me, but if I go with Nana I will have to dress for church, which includes wearing white gloves, which means no chocolate or buttered popcorn, and that's no fun.

I am walking away from the Garden feeling slightly disappointed when I see the first of the red and blue signs. It is tacked to the kiosk by the newspaper stand. I think I see the word "carnival," so I step closer. I read COMING SOON! FRED CARMEL'S FUNTIME CARNIVAL! A FESTIVAL OF FUN. CARNIVAL PARADE — JUNE 25th.

Half a block later I see another sign. FRED CARMEL'S FUNTIME CARNIVAL — RIDES, MIDWAY, PRIZES, SIDESHOW, FOOD FROM MANY NATIONS! ARRIVING JUNE 25th.

And in the next block, two more signs. Fred Carmel's Funtime Carnival will feature a bearded lady, a tattooed man, Pretzel Woman (and more). There will be a Ferris wheel, a roller coaster, a fun house, and a haunted mansion ride.

I have to start saving my money. This sounds even better than when the circus came to Millerton two summers ago.

I look at my watch. It is now 12:10. (My watch is always exactly on time, thanks to Mr. Penny.) Nana will have arrived ten minutes ago. I don't want to go home. But my stomach is growling, and I don't have enough money to buy lunch in town. Also, today is Cookie's pie-baking day.

I jam my hands in my pockets and take the rest of my walk in a big hurry. I call hello to Mr. Shucard in the Meat Wagon, to Mr. Hulit in his shoe store, to old Miss Conroy in Stuff 'n' Nonsense. I wave to Jack, who has just pulled his

Good Humor truck up to the corner, and I tell him maybe I'll see him later. I cross the street at the next intersection, and Miss Julian, Millerton's first lady policeman, says, "Happy summer, Hattie!" I turn left and rush down the other side of Nassau Street, past Papa's law office and the redbrick library. I'm about to run by Clayton's Yarn Shop when Mrs. Winterbotham steps out and catches me by the elbow. "Be a dear, Hattie," she says, "and tell Miss Hagerty her angora is in."

"Okay," I say. I keep on running and am home by 12:25.

I look for signs of Nana. Nothing. No cars in front of the house. Either Nana isn't here after all, or she walked.

I tiptoe inside, closing the screen door silently behind me. I am about to call hello when I hear Nana and Mom in the parlor. They are talking quietly.

"I'm afraid it's going to be the death of Hayden," Nana is saying.

I step on a squeaky floorboard then, and Mom and Nana look up sharply.

"Good afternoon, Hattie," says Nana.

Three

"Hi, Nana," I reply. I wait for the conversation to continue. Which Hayden are they talking about — Papa or Uncle Hayden? And what is going to be the death of him?

Nana acts as if she hasn't just mentioned death. She stands up, a little tottery in her heels, steadies herself on the arm of a chair, and brushes some imaginary wrinkles from the skirt of her dress. "Well, Hattie, are you going to join us for lunch, then?" she asks. I can feel her taking in my shorts, my sandals, my sweaty hair.

I glance at Mom. She looks pained. I know she doesn't care what I wear to lunch, but she doesn't want to contradict her mother. Actually, that's not quite true. Mom will go against Nana's wishes where big enormous things are concerned, like who she marries and what kind of house she lives in. But when it comes to these smaller things — my appearance at lunch when Nana has come over — Mom often gives in. I do not understand this. I think these little things are supposed to be peace offerings, but for what? For running a boardinghouse or for something else, some adult thing I am not part of?

"How about running upstairs and brushing your hair, Hattie?" Mom says finally. A compromise. She will try to please Nana, she will try not to annoy me unduly.

I do this very, very slowly, to demonstrate that it is something of an ordeal after all. When I'm done I tiptoe downstairs, hoping Nana will continue her conversation about the death of Hayden.

I am halfway down the stairs when Dad comes clumping along behind me. I speed up, pretend I wasn't eavesdropping.

"How was downtown, Pumpkin?" he asks me.

"Fine."

"Ready for Nana? Come on, I'll escort you." Dad takes me by the arm, and we walk downstairs together.

Mom and Nana have finished talking and are sitting at the table in the dining room. Nana eyes my father's paint-spattered shirt (he must have switched to the portraits after I left this morning), but she has mostly given up commenting on him. She knows he can be pushed only so far, and she tries to hold her tongue around him.

Dad pretends to be oblivious to Nana. He slides into his chair, reaches for his water glass.

I look around the room. Six places are set at the table. That means Miss Hagerty and Mr. Penny will be eating with us. A few minutes later they arrive. Miss Hagerty drifts in, wafting lavender perfume ahead of her. Mr. Penny rushes in, checking his watch.

Well. We are some group. I know why Nana doesn't eat here very often. For one thing, we are rarely dressed in what she would consider an appropriate fashion. Also, although Nana does get to sit at the head of the table when she visits (unless Papa is with her), no maid magically appears from our kitchen, discreetly offering dishes and bowls, waiting patiently at our elbows while we serve ourselves. And no little buzzer is hidden under the rug by Nana's foot, a buzzer with which she can silently summon the maid from the kitchen.

Mom starts passing around dishes, and we fill our plates. At first no one says anything. We can all feel Nana looking us over. Suddenly we become very aware of our manners. Are our napkins wherever they're supposed to be? Are we keeping one hand in our laps at all times? Mr. Penny checks Miss Hagerty's place to see if he has used the correct fork. I check Dad's plate to see how I am supposed to leave my knife when I am not using it. I know there is some rule.

Nana clears her throat, and the rest of us jump. "Well,"

she says. "Does anybody have any interesting summer plans?"

I don't pay attention to the answers. What I would like to know is why Nana is here in the first place. Nana and Papa rarely come to the boardinghouse for meals. I suspect that Nana's cook has the day off. But surely Nana could have eaten leftovers by herself. No, there is some reason she has come by today, and I think it has to do with whatever it is that's going to be the death of Hayden.

I return to my earlier question: Which Hayden was she talking about? Most likely she meant Papa, since he's much closer to death than Uncle Hayden is. And much closer to us. Uncle Hayden, Mom's older brother, lives in California, and we hardly ever see him.

I am mulling over the things that could cause the sudden death of Papa when I hear Nana utter two words that make my stomach jump, and cause me to put down my fork, stop eating, and pay attention to the conversation. The words are "Summer Cotillion." Nana, in her brightest company voice, is saying, ". . . and I'm on the dance committee. We've been working very hard all spring. We expect this to be a wonderful event. The dance is to be for eleven- and twelve-year-olds."

I can now feel Nana looking at me, so I become intent on spearing exactly one pea with each tine of my fork.

Mom murmurs, "Don't play with your food, honey."

I drop the fork.

"The dance is to be held on the afternoon of July fifteenth, Hattie," says Nana. "That's the day before your birthday. I think attending the cotillion will be a lovely way for you to start celebrating."

I don't answer. Nana knows perfectly well how I feel about dances.

I look to Dad for help. He is serving peas to Miss Hagerty.

I look to Mom for help. "We could get you a new dress," she says.

Miss Hagerty springs to life. "Oh! Oh! I'll make you one!" she cries. "I would love to do that. Who knows, Dearie, maybe you'll find a nice young man at the cotillion."

One of those dresses the Dobie Gillis girls wear could be fun. But I would not dance in it. Not even if Dobie were my partner.

I smile at Miss Hagerty. "Thank you," I say.

There is not a chance I am going to that dance. I missed the Christmas Cotillion because I had strep throat, thank goodness. But I had to go to last year's Summer Cotillion for nine- and ten-year-olds, and it was a horrifying experience. Betsy wasn't there, of course, and for the first hour no one asked me to dance, so I stood by myself, pretending to search for things in my purse, helping out at the punch table even though the chaperones didn't need any help, trying to appear useful instead of ignored. And all the time dreadful Nancy O'Neil and Janet White kept whispering to the boys they were dancing with, and pointing at me. In the second hour of the cotillion one of the boys Janet had danced with asked me to dance, but I think it was some kind of joke, because when it ended Nancy and Janet laughed so hard, they had to get drinks of water from the fountain to keep from choking.

Nana is looking at me, waiting for me to express some ladylike excitement about her cotillion.

I am saved by Miss Hagerty, who says, "Let's go through my patterns this afternoon, Dearie. I'm thinking of a drop waist with a sash, a scoop neck, and long sleeves. Maybe organdy or taffeta?"

"Okay," I say.

After lunch, when we're alone, I can confess to Miss Hagerty that I won't need the dress. And she will understand. She always does.

Mr. Penny, a dreamy look in his eyes, says he remembers a dance back in aught-two, which reminds Miss Hagerty of an old beau, which then reminds Mr. Penny of World War One. Before I know it, the Summer Cotillion is forgotten. And the subject of the death of Hayden has apparently been dropped.

At the end of lunch I escape from the table as quickly as possible.

Four

Half the time I don't know whether to admire my mother or to be furious with her. I suppose I should admire her for being brave enough to stand up to Nana and Papa — for going ahead and marrying Dad when her parents didn't approve of him. Dad, a painter from a middle-class family in the south, with no social credentials to speak of. But he did go to Yale (on a scholarship), and Mom knew Nana would have trouble disapproving of a Mount Holyoke–Yale marriage. The important thing, Mom has told me, is that she knew she and Dad were soul mates. Nothing was going to stop her from spending the rest of her life with him. So they got married and settled in Millerton, and Nana and Papa decided they could tolerate Dad. When Dad couldn't quite make a living with his paintings, he and Mom bought the big house on Grant Avenue and turned it into a boarding-house. Nana's pursed lips whenever she rides down Grant say exactly what she thinks of our house. But Mom ignores Nana. Except for when she gives in to her. Which is about 50 percent of the time.

When Nana leaves after lunch, Mom watches her walk away, says "Huh," under her breath, then pulls a faded kerchief out of her pocket and puts it back on her head so she can help Toby finish the dusting.

I sit on the front porch by myself for a few minutes. I decide to put the cotillion and the death of Papa out of my mind. I spend the rest of the afternoon doing the following: 1. Helping Cookie in the kitchen, for which I am rewarded with a piece of raspberry pie. 2. Helping Mom and Toby with the rest of the cleaning. 3. Lying on my bed and reading from my current stack of library books. 4. Taking Miss Hagerty's afternoon tea tray to her, and explaining why I won't need a new drop-waist organdy dress. 5. Painting with Dad in his studio.

When Dad announces that it is six o'clock and time for dinner, I am honestly surprised. This is why I love summer and don't want to be anywhere but here. All year long I look forward to these days that stretch out endlessly ahead of me, filled with walks and books and painting and Miss Hagerty. And free of class presentations and gym and dances and snippy, gossipy girls. Best of all, when each day ends, the evening still yawns ahead.

We eat dinner together — Mom and Dad, Miss Hagerty, Mr. Penny, Angel Valentine, and I. As soon as the table has been cleared, I glance expectantly at Miss Hagerty.

"Lemonade?" she says.

"Cookie and I made it this afternoon," I reply.

Miss Hagerty looks like she wants to clap her hands and jump up and down. Instead, she says, "I'll wait for you on the porch."

"Lemonade time, is it?" says Mr. Penny. He almost smiles.

And Angel Valentine, who has changed out of her work clothes and is gliding through our dining room in her bare feet, looks at me with interest. "There's lemonade?" she says.

Angel is so wonderful that sometimes I forget she has only lived with us for a month. She doesn't know all our routines.

"In the summer," I tell her, "starting with my first day of vacation, we have lemonade on the porch every night after supper."

The truth is that only Miss Hagerty and I have lemonade on the porch *every* night. Mom and Dad rarely join us, and Mr. Penny joins us if he feels like it. I wonder if Angel Valentine will want to be a part of these summer evenings.

I open the refrigerator, take out the pitcher of lemonade

that Cookie and I made, and set it on a tray with glasses. I carry it carefully to the porch. I am serving Miss Hagerty and Mr. Penny and Angel when I hear Dad say, "Hattie?"

I turn around. Dad is standing at the door, looking at me through the screen. "Can you come inside for a moment?"

I start to say that we are about to have our lemonade, but I am stopped by the tone of Dad's voice. What he has said is not really a question, but an order.

"Okay." I set down my empty glass.

Dad motions me to the parlor, where I see Mom seated on the couch. She is sitting up very, very straight and tall, and looks uncertain, like she is about to have her school picture taken. I am still standing in the doorway when she says, "Hattie, your father and I need to talk to you about something."

I collapse onto a chair. I decide that they are going to make me go to the cotillion.

"This is very serious," Mom adds, and instead I decide that I am about to find out what will be the death of Papa.

"It's Papa, isn't it?" I ask.

"Papa?" Mom repeats. "No, it's . . ." She looks to Dad for help. Dad looks back at her and shrugs his shoulders, a tiny little shrug.

"Hattie, I suppose we should have told you this a long time ago," Mom says.

What? What should they have told me?

Mom has spread her hands in her lap and is touching the knuckles of her left hand with the index finger of her right. She sighs. "Your uncle Hayden and I have another brother," she says at last. "Adam. Your uncle Adam."

"I have another uncle?" I reply. This is especially interesting, since Dad is an only child, and Hayden has never married, so I thought he was my only relative, apart from my grandparents. I have always envied Betsy, who has a total of fourteen aunts and uncles and nearly thirty cousins.

"Yes," Mom replies, still poking at her knuckles, still not looking at me. "Adam is the baby of the family. He was born when I was sixteen, and Uncle Hayden was eighteen."

I do some figuring in my head, and I frown. "Then Uncle Adam is only twenty-one or twenty-two," I say.

"Twenty-one," Mom murmurs.

"Where does he live? Why haven't I ever met him?"

Mom just twists her hands around, so Dad says, "Adam has been away at school. In Ohio. Since he was twelve."

"Twelve?" I am shocked. Who goes away to school when he is twelve and doesn't come back? I do a little more figuring and realize that I was one or two when Adam left. So I probably did meet him, but I would have been too little to remember. "Doesn't he come home for vacations?" I ask.

"Hattie," says Dad, "Adam . . . has some problems."

"What kind of problems?"

"He's not like other people," says Mom.

"What do you mean?"

Another look passes between Mom and Dad. "He has . . . *mental problems*." Dad says the last two words in a loud whisper.

"He's been living at a *special school*." Mom also whispers.

"Then is he retarded?" I ask. This is the way it always is with my family. Twenty questions. I wish my parents could tell me things straight out.

"No, he's not retarded, exactly," Mom answers. "It's that he's not quite . . . right. He has some trouble controlling himself. He's unpredictable, erratic."

"Nana and Papa took him to lots of doctors when he was young," adds Dad. "Some of them thought he was schizophrenic or autistic."

Schizophrenic. Autistic. I don't know these words.

"But why doesn't he come home on school vacations?" I want to know.

"Adam's school isn't like yours, Hattie," says Dad. "He lives there. His teachers know how to manage him."

"But," Mom continues, "his school is about to close. For good. And Adam is coming home to live with Nana and Papa this summer while they look for another school for him. Papa is leaving for Ohio tomorrow. He'll bring Adam back here on Friday."

About eight questions spring to mind. I choose one. It seems to me to be more important than my questions about Adam's illness. "Why didn't anyone ever tell me about Adam? I mean, before now." I am certain I have never heard his name.

Mom, twisting, twisting. Dad, looking like he wishes his hands cupped a glass of Jack Daniel's.

"I guess we just didn't think it was necessary," says Mom.

"We didn't want to worry you," says Dad.

Worry me about what?

They are leaping around the subject as if it were a fire and they were barefoot.

Don't they know how hard it is to be their daughter, to stand by and watch?

Well. I will have to figure things out for myself. I suppose I will meet Adam very soon.

That night I turn out my light at ten o'clock. I lie in bed forever, staring out the window. Sleep will not come.

I am thinking about my new uncle. Adam. I try to picture him.

I hear Mr. Penny's clocks strike eleven, then twelve.

I am still wide-awake.

Finally, I tiptoe downstairs and into the dark parlor. I

turn on a lamp, cross the room to the shelf where we keep our photo albums. I flip through my favorites — the ones with pictures of me when I was little.

But tonight I need different albums, older ones. They haven't interested me before, and so I haven't bothered much with them. Now I open one that is losing its black binding. In it I see Nana and Papa on their wedding day, then Mom and Uncle Hayden as babies. This one is too old. I put it back and locate one in which I find Mom posing for the camera in a cap and gown. Her high school graduation. That's better. I turn a few pages, and there is a photo of Mom and Uncle Hayden, side by side, a small boy standing between them. He is about four years old, and wears perfectly round tortoiseshell glasses. He is leaning forward slightly and giving the camera an enormous grin.

He doesn't look like he has problems.

I pull the photo out of its plastic case and turn it over. In Mom's handwriting I see: Me, Adam, Hayden — 1942.

In the next few pages of photos, Adam grows up quickly. And becomes more and more solemn. I see Adam at five, the round glasses blurring his eyes, standing by a fancy car with Nana and Papa. A year later, a family portrait. Adam is the only one not smiling. He's not looking at the camera either. Mom, standing behind him, is resting a hand on his shoulder. She looks stiff.

What was Adam like when he was a baby? I wonder. What was he like when he was four, six, ten?

And then I wonder for the nine thousandth time that evening why I was never told about Adam. If he didn't have to come home now, would I ever have been told about him?

If a person is kept secret, is he real?

I imagine Nana and Papa and their immaculate home. I try to picture Adam in it. Maybe Nana and Papa think he doesn't fit there. Certainly, he is not part of the perfect world Nana has worked so hard to create.

I'm not perfect either, but luckily I don't live with Nana and Papa.

And then it occurs to me that Mom did. She grew up in that house.

Now that is really something to think about.

Five

Today I am going to meet Adam. Adam Mercer. My new uncle. On Thursday morning Charles the chauffeur drove Papa to the train station in New Liberty so Papa could catch the 6:43 to Cincinnati. Today, which is Saturday, Charles returned to New Liberty to meet the noon train from Cincinnati and brought Papa and Adam (I am having trouble thinking of him as Uncle Adam) home to Nana.

And now Mom and Dad and I are about to leave for dinner at Nana and Papa's. We have already served dinner to Angel Valentine and Mr. Penny and Miss Hagerty, who will be on their own tonight.

It is a warm evening with crickets and birdsongs, so I ask Mom and Dad if we can walk to Nana and Papa's. Then I say, "Mom, when was the last time you saw Adam?"

Mom is at her dressing table, dabbing Chanel Number

Five behind her ears. In the mirror her eyes look at me sharply, then soften. "Why?"

I shrug. "I don't know."

Mom caps the perfume bottle. "It was a long time ago," she says.

That is the end of that discussion.

Twenty minutes later I am wearing my pink and white summer dress, the one with the full skirt, and the rosebuds around the neck, made specially for me by Miss Hagerty. And I am wearing nylons with a garter belt, and my white flats. (Mom and Nana, in agreement for once, say I am not old enough for heels.) In my purse are gloves, in case Nana should look disapprovingly at my bare hands.

Mom and Dad and I cross our lawn and turn left on Grant. I am only a little concerned that we will run into Nancy or Janet, who live nearby and surely are not walking around town in church clothes with their parents. (I'm glad the gloves are in my purse and not on my hands.)

We pass Nancy's house, then Janet's, and no sign of anybody. I relax. But then we reach Nana and Papa's, and suddenly my heart starts to pound.

I am trying to decide whether I should mention this, when the front door flies open and someone cries, "Dorothy! Jonathan! And Hattie! Oh, ho, ho, ho!"

A figure throws itself forward and runs down the walk. It

nearly crashes into Mom before grabbing her in a bear hug. Somewhat to my surprise, I hear Mom say warmly, "Hi, Adam."

"Hi, Dorothy! Hi, Dorothy! Honey, I'm home!" I have never heard anyone speak as fast as Adam. On he goes, a tornado of words. "Jonathan, Jonathan, are you tired rundown listless? Maybe you need Vitameatavegamin, a fine commercial product."

Mom laughs. "Adam, slow down. Have you been watching *I Love Lucy*?"

"Yes, oh yes, *I Love Lucy*, a very funny show. Lucy and Ricky and Fred and Ethel and all their mishaps and antics. Vitameatavegamin, oh, ho, ho, ho!"

I am breathless from listening to Adam.

My parents are smiling. "Adam, you remember Hattie, don't you?" says Dad.

I put my hand out, but Adam ignores it and gives me one of his bear hugs. "My old friend, my old old friend, Hattie Owen, how are you, how old are you? Ethel what birthday is it oh it's mine I meant how old are you going to be she knew what you meant Ricky Ricardo I'm surprised at you it's not nice to ask a woman's age."

Adam is absolutely the strangest person I have ever met, but he is *grinning,* and he is making Mom and Dad and me grin too. My heart has stopped pounding and I feel a little giddy. Christmas morning giddy.

Adam turns and hurries back to the house, beckoning us to follow. We have to run to keep up with him.

"Ermaline has prepared tender roast beef *au jus* with succulent green beans, herbed potatoes, and for dessert, crème caramel," Adam says at high speed.

I try to remember if this is a menu from *I Love Lucy*.

"Adam, Adam, slow down." Nana has hurried into the foyer, Papa just behind her. She puts her hand on Adam's arm. "Slow," she says again.

Adam closes his mouth as if she had said, "Be quiet."

One second later he opens it. "Hattie, Hattie, I have been looking forward to seeing you again. It's been such a long time, too long, far too long. The last time I saw you, you were two years old, no not even two yet, not two, just a baby, a baby really, Hattie."

Papa interrupts. "Let's sit down, everybody. Sherman will bring us drinks in a moment."

"Oh, ho, ho, ho! Drinks! What a good idea!" exclaims Adam.

Mine, I know, will be a Shirley Temple.

Papa motions us into the grand sitting room. We all choose chairs, and I wind up next to Adam. I notice that we settle down rather gingerly, as if something might break. And I do not mean the chairs, but I don't know what I do mean.

Now that he is sitting, Adam has fallen silent. He opens a magazine and begins to read aloud very softly.

I study him. He is small, only a little taller than me, and slight. But wiry. I can see the muscles in his forearms. And he is tense, intense, even when he smiles. His face is so tight that it might jump right off of his head. But apart from that he looks okay. He has two eyes, a nose, a mouth, all in the right spots. Actually, he looks quite a bit like Papa. Except that he leaves his mouth open while he reads and soon his lips glisten with saliva. And he keeps jabbing the round tortoiseshell glasses up the bridge of his nose, although they don't seem to be slipping down.

Sherman appears carrying a tray of drinks in one hand.

"Adam," says Nana, "please put the magazine away."

Adam drops the magazine to the floor as Sherman hands him a drink. Adam leans over to me and whispers, "They always give me a Shirley Temple. What do they give you?"

"I get a Shirley Temple too!"

"Yes, that's the rule, that's the rule when you're a kid, I'm not a kid, but who's counting, how old did you say you are, Hattie?"

I don't get to answer because Papa has risen to his feet and is standing in the middle of the room, holding his glass aloft. His other hand is in his pocket, and he stands straight and stiff as he says, "I propose a toast. Here's to . . . here's to this wonderful occasion on which we can all be together."

I wonder why he doesn't just say, "Here's to Adam."

39

We raise our glasses, then sip from them. And in the next moment I see that Adam has put his whole hand in his glass in order to pull out the cherry that is hiding among the ice cubes.

I just know this is a bad idea.

Sure enough. "Adam!" scolds Nana.

Adam's hand flies out of the glass, showering me with ginger ale.

Nana starts to stand up, but I say, "It's all right. I don't mind." I look at Adam. "It's kind of hot in here. That cooled me off."

Adam's face, which had crumpled as if he were about to burst into tears, now lights up. "Really?"

"Yes. But don't do it again," I whisper, glancing at Nana. Then aloud I say, "I'm going to be twelve on my next birthday."

"Twelve! Twelve years old, imagine that!"

Ermaline has entered the room noiselessly and is whispering to Nana. When she leaves, Nana and Papa start talking about friends of Mom's who are in the middle of a scandalous divorce. Mom and Dad keep glancing at Adam, and Nana keeps asking Mom and Dad questions, pulling their attention back to the conversation. I have seen this before. It's Nana's highly effective and very annoying way of not mentioning the elephant in the living room. But why does she have to think of Adam as an elephant? Why can't he just be their son?

I am not interested in the scandalous divorce, which probably isn't very scandalous anyway. I swish my drink around, cross my feet, uncross them.

I am starting to feel awfully uncomfortable when Adam turns to me and says, "I know when your birthday is, Hattie, yes I do. It's July, July sixteenth. I remember when you were born. What are you going to do on your birthday, Hattie? Will you have a party? Ethel's birthday did not go well, not well at all, she and Lucy had a fight."

"I don't know what I'm going to do," I reply. Now I am trying to figure out if I can get to my own cherry without causing a scene. "I don't really have enough friends for a party."

"Not enough friends? Oh, Hattie, Hattie, that is not possible, not possible at all."

"No, it's true. I only have one friend. Betsy. And she goes away every single summer." Why am I telling Adam these things?

Adam is gazing at me intently. Hardly any grown-up ever pays this much attention to me, except for my parents and Miss Hagerty. But then, Adam doesn't seem like a grown-up, exactly. "Well, this summer your birthday must be special, very special indeed. What do you want for your birthday, Hattie, what sort of present?"

I am thinking about this when Sherman reappears and announces that dinner will be served. We all stand up, and the adults file into the dining room. Adam and I lag behind. "Get your cherry, get it now, Hattie, now while there's still time!" Adam says in a loud whisper.

I do, and then Adam graciously takes me by the elbow and escorts me to my place at the table.

There is dead silence as Ermaline walks around and waits while each of us takes roast beef and green beans and potatoes from the serving dishes. When she leaves I let out a sigh of relief.

We start eating. Adam eats as fast as he talks. I can't stop looking at him. He is sitting across the table from me, and I watch with fascination as he shovels forkful after forkful of food into his mouth. Mostly, he forgets to close his mouth when he chews.

Nana is watching him too. Eventually she says, "Adam, what did we talk about this afternoon? Slow down, please."

Adam glares at his mother. In quick succession he shovels in four more mouthfuls of roast beef, never taking his eyes off of her.

"Adam, party manners," she says quietly.

Adam slams his fist on the table, and every piece of silverware and china jumps. So do I. "Adam, party manners," says Adam in exactly the tone Nana just used. But I notice that he slows down after that.

Also, he stops talking.

I am disappointed. The adults begin discussing a show that is opening in New York City, Nana and Papa speaking a little too fast.

I keep looking at Adam, hoping he'll ask me about my birthday again. Or tell me why he thinks I could be a person with a lot of friends.

But Adam's face has darkened. Later, when dessert is served, Adam picks up his dish of crème caramel with both hands and tries to slurp it down like milk left over from a bowl of cereal.

Papa leaps to his feet. "All right. That does it. Adam —"

Adam doesn't wait to hear anymore. He pushes his chair back from the table and stomps out of the room, in exactly the same way I had wanted to stomp out of the kitchen the other morning.

That is the last I see of Adam on his first day home.

Six

Our family is really not much for church. That is, my parents and I are not. Nana and Papa are a different story. They go absolutely every Sunday. In nice weather, they walk, which means they walk by our house. So the next morning I am not surprised to see them outside in their church clothes at 9:30. But I am surprised to see them stop, then make their way to our porch. And I am quite happy when I realize that Adam is with them, sort of slouching along behind. I open our screen door. "Hello!" I say.

Adam pushes between Nana and Papa. "Hattie! Hattie! Good morning!" he calls. "Good Sunday morning!"

He is dressed in a pale green short-sleeved, button-down cotton shirt with a bright red bow tie, neatly pressed wool pants, and sneakers with white socks. The white socks are just right for the sneakers, but not at all right for the pants, which I think are part of a winter suit. Last night Adam's hair, which is nicely wavy, was parted neatly at one side. This morning he has parted it straight down the middle and slicked it flat with Brylcreem.

"Good morning!" I reply.

Mom joins me on the porch. "Well . . . good morning, everybody," she says. She notices Adam and raises her eyebrows.

"Dorothy," says Nana, "church starts in half an hour, and Adam refuses to go with us. Can he stay here this morning?"

Mom looks at her brother.

"Nope, no thanks, I won't go, no church for me. No church, thank you very much," says Adam.

"Well, can't he just stay at home?" asks Mom.

Dad appears on the other side of the screen door. "What's going on?"

"Let's go inside," Mom whispers to Nana and Papa, as if Adam weren't standing just two feet away from her.

Nana and Papa follow Mom into the house. Adam looks at me. "Where's Miss Hagerty?" he asks.

"Miss Hagerty? You know her?" I say.

"Yes, oh yes, lovely lady, lovely lady indeed. Does she still live here? Oh, maybe she died, maybe she has passed on, gone over, she must be eighty, maybe ninety, maybe more than ninety."

"Good Lord in heaven, I have a long way to go before I

turn ninety, young man." Miss Hagerty bustles onto the front porch, clutching her knitting bag.

"Miss Hagerty, Miss Hagerty, oh, ho, ho, ho! You *are* here! They said you would be, but I had to see with my own eyes."

Adam gives Miss Hagerty one of his hugs, and they sit down on the porch swing together.

"Do you know Mr. Penny too?" I ask Adam. This is fascinating.

"Mr. Penny, Mr. Penny, why of course I know Mr. Penny, the White Rabbit, late, always late, checking his watch, repairing his clocks. Late, late, late and hurry, hurry, hurry. Where is he? Frankly Mrs. Ricardo you've contracted a terrible terrible attack of the gabloots. Gabloots?! Doctor what kind of a disease is that well we doctors don't know too much about it but there's a terrible epidemic of it lately —"

I rush to stop Adam before he gets carried away. "Would you like to see Mr. Penny too? He's right upstairs. I can go get him."

"Yes, oh yes, and fine, fine, fine."

I am wondering if Miss Hagerty is going to be all right alone with Adam, when she looks up from her knitting and says to him, "So tell me everything."

I intend to run straight upstairs to Mr. Penny's room. I

really do. But I can't help stopping to listen outside the parlor for a moment.

"Adam is not a baby, Mother," Mom is saying. "He's almost twenty-two years old. Can't he stay at home alone?"

"He's your own brother, Dorothy," Papa says. "Is he not welcome here?"

"Of course he's welcome here. It's not that. He's welcome here any time. I just don't understand why . . . don't you think Adam is a bit old to need baby-sitting? He's a grown man after all."

"I am aware of his age," Nana replies. "But it's too soon to leave him to his own devices. He's still getting used to everything."

My mother lets out a sigh.

I hear Papa say, "Church starts in twenty minutes."

Dad steps in quickly. "It's fine if he stays here this morning."

I step back from the parlor and run upstairs to Mr. Penny's room. I knock on his door and tell him who's downstairs. "He says he wants to see you," I add.

"Adam Mercer. My stars. I'll come down as soon as I can."

I reach the first floor just as Nana and Papa are about to leave.

"Wait, everybody!" says Dad suddenly. "Let me get the movie camera."

"Jonathan, we're going to be late," says Papa.

My father is already rushing down the hallway, calling that it's a beautiful day and Nana and Papa are in their nice church clothes.

A few minutes later, Nana, Papa, Adam, Mom, Miss Hagerty, and I are lined up on the porch steps, squinting into the sun. "Wave at the camera!" calls Dad, and we all do, except for Adam who seems to have gone deaf, and just keeps squinting.

Then Nana and Papa rush off.

"We'll see you in a couple of hours, Adam," calls Papa.

"Mind your party manners," adds Nana.

Mom and Dad chat with Adam and Miss Hagerty and me until they have to start getting lunch ready. When they leave, I glance gratefully at Miss Hagerty. I don't know how I would feel, what Adam and I would talk about, if we were left by ourselves. But Miss Hagerty can talk a blue streak, as she often says. And I am glad.

Miss Hagerty is asking Adam something about *I Love Lucy,* when Mr. Penny steps onto the porch. Adam leaps to his feet. "There he is! There he is! Mr. Penny, my dear friend, it's been such a long time. How's your shop, how are the clocks, how are the cuckoos?"

The corners of Mr. Penny's eyes crinkle a little, which is as good as a smile. "Well, the shop is closed now, Adam, but the clocks are fine."

I wonder if Adam doesn't feel like Rip Van Winkle, greeting these people he hasn't seen in so many years.

"The shop is closed, closed now, is it? Well, that is something. My, my, my."

Miss Hagerty and Mr. Penny talk quietly with Adam, and after a few minutes I realize that he isn't speaking quite as fast as before. Everything about him has slowed down.

Mr. Penny is telling Adam about his grandfather clock and how I wind it so faithfully each week, when Miss Hagerty looks at her watch and struggles to her feet. "Goodness sake!" she says. "Adam, I must leave for church. I'm sorry to cut our visit short."

Miss Hagerty is one of Millerton's Presbyterians. Nana and Papa are Episcopalians. (Mom and Dad call them Presbies and Episkies.) The Presbies worship later in the morning than the Episkies do. Mom and Dad say we can worship anytime we please by sending messages to God with our minds, which, also we don't need a fancy building for.

Miss Hagerty leaves with two other old ladies who pick her up in their brown Chrysler. Mr. Penny drifts back inside. Adam and I are alone on the porch. I realize Adam is staring at me.

"Hattie," he says at last, looking thoughtful, "I believe you are one of the people who can lift the corners of our universe."

A slow smile spreads across my face. I feel very flattered, even though I have absolutely no idea what Adam means by that.

"Well, thank you. I —" I start to say.

"Morning, Hattie." I am interrupted by a sleepy voice on the other side of the screen door.

Angel Valentine is standing there in a pale summer dress, looking lovely and not all the way awake. I have never known a grown-up who sleeps as late as Angel Valentine does on the weekends.

"Hi," I say. "Angel, this is Adam. He's my uncle."

Adam has swiveled around to look at Angel. Now he jumps to his feet. He becomes a blur of motion, wiping his hands on his pants, scraping his shoes on the porch floor, pushing his glasses up his nose, and extending his arm as if to shake Angel's hand right through the screen.

"Adam, this is Angel Valentine. She just moved here last month," I say. "She has a job with a bank and one day she's going to work in a big city like Philadelphia or New York."

"Hey, hey, oh, hey, oh, all right," Adam stammers. His face has turned scarlet. "Ho, *ho!*"

Adam plunges forward to get the door for Angel and pushes it several times before realizing he needs to pull it. Then he swings it open with one hand and tremulously ushers Angel onto the porch with the other.

"Thank you," says Angel Valentine in her husky voice. "God, it's hot today." She ambles to the porch railing and looks toward Grant Avenue. She is barefoot and smells of shampoo and toothpaste.

Adam can't take his eyes off of her. "You work in a bank, work in a bank, do you?" Suddenly he is at top speed again. "Lucy now look I'm serious I don't know what's the matter with you every month every single month your bank account is overdrawn now what is the reason?"

Angel Valentine looks puzzled for a moment, then laughs. "Oh! That's from *I Love Lucy*. The one when Lucy and Ethel get jobs in the chocolate factory, isn't it?"

Adam positively beams. "Yes, oh yes. That's the one. One of the best, one of the very best."

Angel yawns. "I guess I missed breakfast, didn't I, Hattie?"

I love Angel Valentine for not seeming to notice that there is anything unusual about Adam.

I nod. "But when Miss Hagerty gets back from church it will be time for lunch."

"Okay." Angel lets herself back into the house. "Nice to meet you, Adam. I'll see you later."

"Yeah, I'll see you later," Adam echoes. He presses himself to the screen door and watches Angel until she disappears into the upstairs hallway. Then he begins pacing back and forth across the porch. "My, my. Boy, oh boy, oh boy, oh boy. Hey, Hattie, Hattie," he says without looking in my direction, "when was the last time you were on a train? A train, Hattie. They have sleeping cars, you know, with berths, and quite good food, good food on the trains, Hattie." Adam is smiling, excited.

I watch him. Adam is something of a train himself, I think, barreling along. He can come to a screeching stop, though, at any moment. I know because I saw it happen last night at dinner.

I am thinking about dinner and Adam and his moods, when I realize Adam is saying, "Oh, ho, ho, ho, Hattie! Are these friends of yours?"

I jerk to attention and look toward the street. There are Nancy and Janet, dressed in fresh skirts and blouses, pocketbooks over their arms, probably on their way back from church. They have paused at the end of our walk, arms linked. They gape at Adam.

"Good morning, good morning, and how do you do!" calls Adam.

The girls do not answer. But I think I can see the edges of smiles on their lips. Nancy pokes Janet in her side, and Janet pokes her back.

"Hattie, are these friends of yours, are they? Come on, come visit us, come join us. We could offer you some lemonade, some zesty lemonade, fresh from the country kitchen."

Nancy and Janet put their hands to their mouths, which does absolutely nothing to hide their giggles. It occurs to me that they must not be getting much out of their churchgoing. They turn and run. I hear their laughter all the way to the corner.

Adam has sagged into a chair. He looks at me. I think maybe he is going to cry. Instead he gives me a small smile and says, "And they went wee, wee, wee, all the way home."

Seven

Ever since the day I found out Adam was coming home I have been busier than usual. Today I finally have time to chat with my friends downtown. I sit beside Mr. Shucard in the Meat Wagon for a while, and he lets me ring up two customers. Mr. Hulit is very busy in the shoe store, so I don't stay long, but Miss Conroy is having a slow day. "Can I help you with anything?" I ask her, and she gives me a whole box of china animals that need price stickers on their bottoms. When I leave Stuff 'n' Nonsense I see Jack at his usual corner. I buy a strawberry shortcake ice-cream bar and tell him about my new uncle. "He might be here all summer," I say, "so you'll probably get to meet him." Jack has heard about Adam, of course. There's not a soul in Millerton who hasn't heard this piece of gossip.

I set off down the street again. Fred Carmel's Funtime Carnival signs are everywhere now, advertising cotton candy and bearded ladies and rides and prizes and more, always more, I absolutely cannot wait for Saturday.

There is a no-food-or-drink rule at the library, which makes sense, so I wait until I have finished my ice cream before I visit Mrs. Moore. When I leave the library, my arms are full of books about Betsy and Eddie, and also Betsy and Tacey, and briefly I think how lucky Betsy McGruder is with her name. I can't think of many book characters named Hattie.

I am hurrying along Grant with my books when I see someone on our front porch, waving frantically.

Adam.

"Hattie! Ho, ho!" he shouts.

"Hi, Adam," I call. "What —" I almost say, "What are you doing here?" but realize that sounds rude, so instead I say, "Where's Nana? Is she here too?"

"Nana, Nana, no, no, no. I came here by myself, by myself, yes indeed. I came for a little walk, and to see the lovely Miss Angel Valentine, is she here?"

"Angel?" I repeat. "No, she's at work. She works at the bank, remember?"

"Yes, oh yes, like the teller in *I Love Lucy*. What do you have there, Hattie? What's all that?"

"I went to the library." I am showing Adam my books

when I hear the phone ring. "I'll get it!" I cry. Although I don't know why I bother to feel excited since unless Betsy is around, the phone is never for me. "Be right back," I say to Adam.

I run inside and pick up the phone in the hallway. "Hattie?" says Nana's voice when I answer. "Is Adam there?" She sounds breathless.

"Yes. He's —"

"Oh, thank goodness."

"Didn't you know he was coming here?" I ask.

"No! He left without telling me. I wasn't even sure he remembered the way to your house."

"Well, he's here. I don't know how long he's been here. I just got back from downtown and found him standing on our porch."

"May I speak to him, please?"

Uh-oh. Nana's tone of voice makes me picture Adam with his hand in his drink.

I call Adam to the phone and listen to his end of the conversation: "Yes? . . . Yes. . . . Okay . . . but I know the way like the back of my hand, the back of my hand." All very calm. And then, "I don't have to tell you everything. . . . No, I am not coming home! Not now, not when Hattie is showing me her books. . . . I am not a baby, Mother!" Adam tries to throw the phone to the floor, but the cord won't reach. He leaves it dangling and slams his way onto the front porch.

I pick up the receiver. "Nana? I was thinking. Could Adam stay here for a little while? We're going to have lunch soon. I could walk him home after that."

"All right." A big resigned sigh. But I hear something else in that sigh. Relief, maybe.

So Adam stays for lunch that day. He is disappointed to find out that Angel Valentine does not come back to the boardinghouse for lunch, but he recovers, and seems to enjoy spending time with Mom and Dad and Miss Hagerty and Mr. Penny and me.

After lunch Adam and I sit on the porch, and now he's serious and thoughtful. Adam's moods are like a deck of playing cards with someone riffling through them — dozens of cards, one after the other, in a blur.

"The whole world passes by your house, Hattie," Adam says after a moment. He's looking toward Grant Avenue.

"I know. That's why sometimes I hate our porch." When Adam looks at me sharply, I hasten to add, "I mean, I don't really hate our porch —"

"You can hate your porch," says Adam.

"Good. Because sometimes I do."

Adam is still just looking at me, waiting.

"Some days," I say, "I feel like I don't belong anywhere in that world. That world out there." I point to Grant. "People walk down our street and people drive down it and people ride their bicycles down it and all of them, even the ones I know, could be from another planet. And I'm a visiting alien."

"And aliens don't belong anywhere," Adam finishes for me, "except in their own little corners of the universe."

"Right," I say.

Later, Adam seems happy to let me walk him home. He loops his arm through mine and sings, "Oh, mares eat oats and does eat oats and little lambs eat ivy." He stops singing before we reach his front door. "You've told me one of your secrets, Hattie, and soon I'll tell you one of mine," he says. Then he opens the door and disappears into the cool darkness of Nana and Papa's house.

Eight

On Tuesday I am just about to set off for downtown when Adam comes whistling up our front walk. "Hattie! Hattie! A great good morning to you!" he calls.

I slip inside and telephone Nana right away to let her know Adam is here, and she is grateful but doesn't ask to speak with him.

When I return to the porch, Adam says, "Is Angel here? Is Angel Valentine at home?"

"No, she's at the bank," I remind him. "Her job." And then I realize that maybe Adam doesn't know much about jobs. So I add, "She leaves every morning before nine o'clock and she comes back every afternoon just a little after five."

"Well, that's a fine how-do-you-do," Adam grumbles, but he doesn't seem terribly upset. He leaps to his feet. "I must be on my way then. Tally ho and adieu."

"Wait, Adam! Where are you going?"

"Home, James," he replies, and sets off down Grant.

I tail Adam all the way back to Nana and Papa's, like a spy, to make sure he doesn't do anything weird when he's walking around town. Then I tear on home and phone Nana to tell her what I've done and that Adam knows his way home just fine.

I feel a little like Adam's baby-sitter, a little like his mother, not at all like his niece, and quite a bit like his friend.

The next day, Adam shows up at our house at precisely 5:05 P.M. (This time I don't bother to call Nana.) Ten minutes later, while he and I are watching Miss Hagerty swish those knitting needles of hers around, Angel Valentine turns up our walk.

Adam is on his feet in an instant. "Angel Valentine! Oh, ho, ho, ho! A great good evening to you. How was your day at the bank?"

Angel collapses into a chair, fanning herself. "It was fine, Adam, thank you. Very busy."

Adam can't take his eyes off of Angel. I watch them travel from her face all the way down to her feet, then up again to settle on her chest. Miss Hagerty is occupied with her knitting needles, and Angel has closed her eyes briefly, so I am the only one watching Adam watch Angel. He is rocking back and forth, from one foot to the other, wringing his hands, and . . . just staring at her bosom.

Angel opens her eyes and sees Adam. I cringe, but she smiles at him. Then she stands up. "I think I'll make some iced tea before dinner," she says. "Does anybody else want any?"

"Oh! Oh! I'll help you! I'll help you in the kitchen, Angel Valentine! Honey what are you doing now mixing in the eggs oil vinegar eggs why don't you put some anchovies make a Caesar salad?"

Angel holds the door open for Adam. "Which *I Love Lucy* is that from?" she asks as they disappear down the hall toward the kitchen.

I feel a flush start in my cheeks as I watch Adam hurry after Angel. I know he has been waiting for days to see her again. I try to tell myself that this is okay; that Adam is a grown man and Angel is a grown woman — a beautiful grown woman. It wouldn't be right for him to look at me the way he looked at Angel. I am only eleven years old, not to mention his niece. But that flush won't go away, and I stare out at Grant Avenue in confusion.

There is nothing like feeling left out.

On Thursday I try not to think about Adam. I take my walk into town. I paint with Dad in his studio. I lie on my bed and read a library book. I help Cookie in the kitchen. Finally

I realize that I miss Adam. So I feel a happy flutter in my stomach when I hear him come whistling up our front walk late that afternoon. I run outside to meet him.

"Ho, ho, and good afternoon, Hattie," says Adam. He's all dressed up, wearing a too-small summer suit with a lime green bow tie and a broad black felt hat, so I think he's expecting to see Angel again. But he doesn't ask about her. Instead, he plops down in a porch chair, crosses one leg over the other, regards me seriously, and says, sounding as if we might be in a business meeting, "Very well. You shared one of your secrets with me, Hattie Owen. Now I'll share one of mine with you."

"Okay," I reply, trying to catch up with Adam. Sometimes I feel that he is miles ahead of me.

"Give me a date, Hattie, any date," says Adam.

"A date?"

"Yes. A month and a day and a year. January seventh in the year nineteen fifty-two, for example."

I think for a moment. Then I say, "Okay. September sixteenth, nineteen forty-one."

"Tuesday," says Adam promptly.

"What do you mean?"

"September sixteenth nineteen forty-one was a Tuesday."

"How do you know?"

"I just do. It's in my head."

"Are you sure you're right?"

"Positive. You can look the date up. Give me another one. A date that you know."

Well, I happen to know what day of the week Cookie was born on, so I give Adam Cookie's birth date.

"Saturday," says Adam.

"That's right!"

Adam is grinning like a Halloween pumpkin.

"You can really do this with any date at all?"

"Absotively."

"How come it's a secret?"

Adam leans forward and whispers loudly, "Because Mother says it's a circus trick and it's embarrassing and it must be kept in the family. The bosom of the family, I might add, although Mother didn't say that."

No, I can't imagine Nana saying "bosom" under any circumstances.

"So there you have it," says Adam, settling back in his chair and looking satisfied.

I have missed something. "What?" I say.

Adam's eyes grow unfocused. He glances away, then back at me, then away again. "My little corner of the universe," is all he will say.

Early Friday morning I am on my way to Miss Hagerty's room with her breakfast tray when I pause at our front door.

The weather forecast has called for rain, but I don't see a single cloud.

What I do see, though, almost causes me to drop the tray.

It is Adam. He is walking jauntily down Grant, wearing his pajama bottoms and nothing more. No shirt, no shoes.

My heart pounds faster, and I draw in a sharp breath. Then I set the tray on the floor and dash outside and down the walk. Adam has already passed our house. I turn right, calling, "Adam! Adam!"

Adam stops walking and swivels around. "Ho, ho! And a great good morning to you, Hattie Owen! A great good morning, a good morning to be alive. Alive, alive, oh! Alive, alive, oh! Cockles and mussels, alive, alive, oh! Do you know that song, do you, Hattie?"

Adam is grinning, a grin that splits his face. This is the best mood I have ever seen him in.

I catch up with him and take his hand. "Adam, where are you going?"

"Where am I going? Where am I going, you ask? Why, I am on my way to the circus of life, the circus of life, Hattie, and I would be honored and delighted, D-E-lighted, if you would accompany me."

Adam has not slowed down. He is continuing in the direction of town, moving so fast that I have to run to keep up with him. How do I make him turn around? He must come with me; I'll take him back to Nana and Papa. But I don't know how to turn him around.

I am a little afraid of making him mad.

I think about what he said, about the circus of life. Has he seen the carnival posters? Is that what he's talking about?

"I do want to go to the circus with you, Adam," I say. "But it isn't here yet. The carnival, I mean. It doesn't get here until tomorrow. Fred Carmel's Funtime Carnival."

"Yes, oh yes. The famous Fred Carmel and his Funtime Carnival. Fun, fun, fun for everyone."

"So let's turn around, then," I say. "We can go to the carnival next week."

I stop, and tug at Adam's arm. For one second I feel him resist, and I think, What will I do if he won't come with me? What will Adam do if he gets mad?

But the next thing I know, Adam has turned and we are walking back toward our house. Adam slows his pace, and soon we are ambling along, like we are just any old people out for an early morning walk, except that one of them is wearing only his striped pajama bottoms.

We pass our house, and I wonder if I should run inside and wake up Mom and Dad, or at least pick Miss Hagerty's tray up from the floor, but I don't want to disturb things with Adam. Better just to return him to Nana and Papa.

So we keep walking, arm in arm now. Silently.

And it dawns on me that we will have to pass by Nancy's house, then Janet's.

Okay. I will just pray to that god of my parents, the one who is always listening — pray that Nancy and Janet will be inside their houses sound asleep as we pass by.

Apparently God is taking a break and doesn't hear me, because as Adam and I approach Nancy's house the front door opens and Nancy runs outside, chasing after her little brother. She chases him across their lawn and to within ten feet of Adam and me before she sees us. When she does, she screeches to a halt and stares.

"Well, and good morning to you, friend of Hattie," says Adam. "Friend who does not want lemonade. Friend who has a baby brother." He salutes Nancy. "Would you like to come home with us and have some savory breakfast sausage?"

Nancy's mouth is hanging open. "No," she manages to say.

Well. Just plain no.

I know Adam looks funny and all, but couldn't Nancy at least be polite to him?

Adam, hurt, turns away.

And I hear Nancy mutter, "You big freak."

I let go of Adam's hand and I spin around. "Hey!" I say. "Hey . . ." I am not very good at insults. "Hey, shut up."

It's not much, but since Nancy has barely heard me say

two words in all the time we've known each other, she looks surprised — and shuts up.

"Come on, Adam," I say.

We walk the rest of the way in silence. And we do not run into Janet. By the time we reach Nana and Papa's, I see that tears are sliding down Adam's cheeks. I ring the doorbell, my heart starting to flutter.

Ermaline appears, then finds Nana in a hurry. I tell Nana what happened. And even though Adam is still crying in that silent way, she says to him, "Now you march right upstairs, young man, and put on some proper clothes." But she sounds more shocked than mad.

Adam heads for the stairs. When he is gone from sight, I say, "Nancy O'Neil called Adam a big freak. He heard her."

Nana stands before me, as straight as a rod, her posture perfect. Nothing in her face moves. If Adam has been insulted, then Nana has been insulted. I can read her eyes as if they are a library book. Nana, one of the wealthiest people in Millerton, expected a perfect family, a family who would live up to the high standards set by Nana's father. But her children have failed her, which means Nana has failed.

"I have to go," I say, and I leave to have breakfast with my own family. I try not to remember Adam's quiet tears.

Nine

I wake up on Saturday morning with butterflies in my stomach. Today Fred Carmel's Funtime Carnival will arrive. Adam will not get to see it. Nana and Papa have chosen this day to take Adam to Philadelphia for some new clothes. I'm sorry Adam will miss the parade, but glad that Nana has noticed things like his too-small summer suit. I wonder who was in charge of Adam's clothes while he was away at school. I think that maybe Nana didn't care what he looked like when he was out of her sight. And then I tell myself to stop thinking mean thoughts about Nana.

"Imagine, a parade right down your street, Hattie," says Cookie as I help her in the kitchen after breakfast. We are both wearing aprons (made by Miss Hagerty), and Cookie has pulled her hair back with a net. Also, she has rolled her stockings down to just below her knees. It is not a good look, but Cookie is fanning herself and sweating, and swears to God in heaven that the rolled-down stockings make her feel ten degrees cooler.

I think of Fred Carmel's posters. Several of them advertise that when the carnival arrives, the wagons and trucks and trailers will parade through town on their way to the carnival site. They will start on Nassau Street, then turn onto Grant and follow Grant to the other side of Millerton.

"Who are you going to watch the parade with?" Cookie asks me.

"Well, you know, Mom and Dad, Mr. Penny and Miss Hagerty. Angel, if she's around. And you, if you want to watch."

"No one your own age?"

I cross my arms. "Betsy is in Maine," I remind her.

"Is Betsy the only other eleven-year-old in Millerton?"

"No."

Cookie smiles at me and puts her arms out. I step away. She sighs. "Oh, honey," she says.

"Well, you sound like Mom."

"Your mother just wants you to have friends."

"I *do* have friends."

"Friends your own age."

"Why does it matter how old my friends are?"

Cookie sighs again. "I suppose it doesn't."

We are baking muffins, and I am filling the muffin tins with our batter. We work without speaking for a few minutes. Finally I decide I don't want Cookie to think I'm mad at her, so I say, "*Will* you watch the parade with us?"

"For a few minutes," she replies. "Long enough to see some of those sideshow people."

It is not yet ten o'clock that morning when I hear shouts and some tinkly music. I run to the porch and look down our street. I see a long line of trucks and wagons moving slowly. I dash back inside.

"It's here!" I shout. "The parade is coming."

Everyone rushes to the porch and sits on the chairs I've lined up in front of the railing. Miss Hagerty is so excited, she squeezes my hand.

The first truck in the parade is painted like a circus wagon. Red letters outlined in gold announce FRED CARMEL'S FUNTIME CARNIVAL. Two young women dressed in spangly costumes sit atop the wagon and wave to us. (Miss Hagerty waves back.) The tinkly music is coming from somewhere inside the wagon. Next come several trailers containing animals, and behind them trot three ponies, each led by a carnival woman in a spangly costume.

"Oh, there they are!" Cookie cries suddenly.

"Who?" asks Angel.

"The sideshow people."

I see that the next few trailers are like commercials for the sideshow. Each one announces one of the sideshow attractions — Man of a Thousand Tattoos; Mongo the Ape Man; John-Jane, Half Man–Half Woman; Pretzel Woman; Mr. Geek — but these people must be inside their trailers. All we get to see are their advertisements.

Cookie is rising to her feet, shaking her head slowly. "My, my. I have to get me to that sideshow," she says as she makes her way back to the kitchen.

I stare at the next trailers that snake down our street, but I don't pay much attention to them. I am thinking of Mongo and John-Jane and Pretzel Woman. I have to admit that I am fascinated by their pictures, the ones on the sides of their trailers. But a tiny part of me feels uncomfortable. If I were unusual looking or had a strange talent, would I want to spend my life being gawked at by everyone who has paid his quarter to see the show? Probably not. And yet . . . I am awfully curious, especially about John-Jane. I decide finally that I am 85 percent curious and only 15 percent uncomfortable.

And when the parade ends I am buzzy with excitement. I try to remember how much money I have upstairs. I think I have forty-five cents in the dish on top of my desk, and nearly five dollars inside the left leg of the jeans in my third bureau drawer. Perfect. I am ready for midway games and cotton candy and shows of any sort.

"Well, Hattie," said Dad. "What do you say? Shall we go to the carnival on Monday night?"

"Monday night? The first night?" I exclaim. "Oh, yes!"

That evening after supper Dad and I walk along Grant all the way to the other side of town and watch Fred Carmel and his workers setting up the carnival. I am amazed at how quickly they work. The empty field is already transformed. Rides are being erected, tents and booths and concession stands have sprung up.

"The grand opening is Monday night," says a girl about my age as she steps out of a trailer.

"We'll be there," Dad replies.

The carnival is the biggest event Millerton has seen in years. It turns out that absolutely everyone in our house is going to attend the grand opening. Mom can't decide whether to serve Monday night dinner half an hour early in order to give people extra time at the carnival, or half an hour late in order to give people time to get ready for it first. In the end, she decides not to change the time.

The six of us sit at the dining room table chattering away about the things we will see and do at Fred Carmel's and how late we might stay up. Mom actually says to me, "Don't eat too much dinner tonight, Hattie. Save room for cotton candy."

"And for the food from many nations," I add. Then I ask, "Can we take Adam to the carnival with us?" I am pretty sure he won't be going with Nana and Papa. A carnival would be beneath them, just as the circus was beneath them.

"Oh, honey," says Mom. "Let's go by ourselves, the three of us. I don't really feel like calling Nana right now."

"I'll call her," I say.

Mom sighs. "Hattie, leave it alone."

"All *right*." I am not going to make a scene in front of everyone. But I know what's going on. Mom doesn't want Nana to know that we are as excited as the rest of the Millerton commoners who are rushing off to the opening night of bearded ladies, midway games, cheap prizes, and glitzy lights.

Well. I am not going to let this spoil my evening.

The moment dinner is over, Miss Hagerty zips out to the front porch. About two minutes later the brown Chrysler pulls up, Miss Hagerty's friends side by side in the front seat. They wave out the windows. Both are wearing straw hats decorated with artificial flowers.

"Yoo-hoo!" they cry.

"Hellooo!" Miss Hagerty replies. "We'll be right there." She turns and calls through the front door, "Frank!" and Mr. Penny appears.

He and Miss Hagerty hurry down our walk together and ease themselves into the car. When I was little I used to think that Mr. Penny and Miss Hagerty were dating and that one day they would get married and I would be the flower girl in their wedding. Now I am pretty sure that neither one of them is meant to get married. That's just the way it is for some people.

No sooner has the Chrysler disappeared from view than a snappy little red convertible car, top down, roars to a stop at the end of our walk. A grinning young guy who looks exactly like Frankie Avalon the singing star gets out of the car without bothering to open the door; just jumps over the side and lands neatly in the street. I stare at him with my mouth open as he walks around to the passenger door and leans against the car, arms folded. I have never seen him before, but I just know he has arrived to pick up Angel Valentine. Sure enough, a few moments later Angel breezes onto the porch, trailing the scent of roses behind her.

"See you later, Hattie," she says. "Have fun tonight."

Frankie Avalon greets Angel with a brush of his lips across her cheek, then holds the car door open for her. A few minutes later they are zooming toward the carnival.

This is one of those moments when I love our porch. Sometimes sitting on it is better than going to the movies.

Mom and Dad and I walked to the carnival. I am so excited that I do not mind holding hands with them even though we are in public. I step along, my right hand in Mom's, my left in Dad's, listening to their quiet voices crisscross above my head. I have forgotten all about Mom and Nana and Nana's airs. But I have not forgotten about Adam. I still wish he could come with us.

I hear Fred Carmel's before I see it, hear music and laughter and a quiet roar of voices. And as we cross a field of parked cars, I see that practically every inch of the carnival is outlined in lights. It looks like Nassau Street in December when store windows and wreaths and lampposts and trees are ablaze for Christmas.

I stand on tiptoe for a better view, and see a moving circle of light, a Ferris wheel. An alley of lights is the midway, another is the sideshow. There is a lit-up bumper car ride, a lit-up Whirl-About, and the snaking lights of a small roller coaster.

Mom and Dad are as excited as I am. "Come on!" says Mom, and she pulls my hand and the three of us run the rest of the way through the parking lot to the entrance. And then . . . we don't know where to start. Food? Rides? Games? The sideshow? So for a while we just walk around.

Then, all of a sudden, Dad's camera is in front of his face. "Okay, ladies," he says to Mom and me. "Stand over there and wave."

We stand in front of the fun house and wave obediently at Dad.

"Now let me film you getting on the Ferris wheel," he says.

Our carnival evening has begun. When we get off of the Ferris wheel we go through the fun house. Then we buy cotton candy. Then I spend four dollars playing six different games before I win a small pink teddy bear.

We stand in line to buy tickets to the sideshow and who should take our money but the girl Dad and I met on Saturday night.

"She *works* here," I whisper incredulously to Dad.

I am still 85 percent fascinated by the thought of the sideshow attractions, and only 15 percent uncomfortable. By the time we are halfway through them, however, I decide I am 15 percent uncomfortable, 45 percent fascinated, and 40 percent disappointed. I think that some of the people are not quite what they were advertised to be. For instance, the woman with the horrifyingly embarrassing name of Pig Lady, billed as the fattest lady in the world, doesn't look any fatter to me than Mrs. Finch who owns the Garden Theater. John-Jane, the Half Man–Half Woman, looks to me like an entire man who just let his hair grow longer on one side of his head than the other, and who stuffed one side of his shirt with wadded-up hand towels, the way Betsy and I do when we want to see how we will look when we get bosoms. (We stuff both sides of our shirts, of course.) And Pretzel

Woman is not actually able to tie herself in knots, although the fact that she can put both her legs around the back of her neck is impressive.

It is after ten o'clock when Mom looks at her watch and says, "I hate to say this, but we should think about heading home. It's pretty late."

"Could we have one more ride on the Ferris wheel?" I ask.

Mom and Dad look at each other. "Why not?" says Mom.

So we take one more ride, watching the carnival fall away from us, then rise to meet us, over and over. When we finally alight, tired and happy and just a little dizzy, I see the girl again, the one who took our tickets at the sideshow.

"I hope you enjoyed your ride," she calls after us. "Come again!"

When I turn around, she waves to me.

I wave back.

Jen

You never know when you're going to find a new friend.
It can happen when you're least expecting it. Betsy and I be-
came friends in kindergarten because Miss Kushel changed
the seating arrangement in our room and Betsy and I wound
up next to each other.

Adam came crashing into my life without warning, and
somehow understood about porches and feeling alien, and
trusted me with his secret.

But Leila may have been my most unexpected friend of
all. She wasn't already in my life — wasn't in my kindergarten room, wasn't an unknown relative. She was just a girl
traveling with a carnival that happened to come to town.

The night Mom and Dad and I go to the opening of Fred
Carmel's I come home exhausted but I can't fall asleep. I lie

in bed and think about Pig Lady and John-Jane and Pretzel Woman, and then I find myself remembering the girl with the dark brown eyes who took our tickets and hoped we enjoyed our ride and told us to come again.

I am still thinking about her the next morning when I begin my walk into town. I don't get any farther than the movie theater when I see the first of the Fred Carmel signs and in a flash I have turned around and am heading back through Millerton to the carnival grounds.

The carnival in the daytime is lots of fun but not as magical as it is at night when it is all lit up and anything, anything at all, might happen. I walk through the midway, then by the food stands, jingling the change that is in my pocket, and feeling the sun strong on my shoulders.

I can't help it. After fifteen minutes I am standing at the entrance to the sideshow again, reading all those signs, looking at the faces of John-Jane and Pig-Lady.

From nearby I hear a woman say, "Let's go to the freak show now!" and she grabs the hand of a man and joins the line of people waiting to buy tickets. I peer into the ticket booth, and there's the girl again. She is busily making change. I have enough money in my pocket for a ticket, but I decide not to buy one. I am thinking of Adam on the day I ushered him home in his pajama bottoms, and of the look on his face when Nancy called him a big freak. Instead, I buy a hot dog and go home.

But the next day when it is time for my walk I head straight for Fred Carmel's again. This time I avoid the sideshow. I have one dollar in my pocket and maybe I will win another prize. I am eighty cents through the dollar, and in the middle of a nerve-racking ringtoss game, when I see the girl. She ducks behind the counter and whispers something to the man who has been taking all my ringtoss money. He hands her a roll of dimes, and she thanks him. She is about to leave when she notices me tossing the rings. She waves shyly at me, and I wave back. Then she runs off.

On Thursday I make a beeline for the carnival as soon as my chores are done. As I run by Nana and Papa's house I consider stopping in and asking Adam to go to the carnival with me, but I have not been in charge of Adam all by myself, except for walking him home, and I'm not sure I'm ready for that. Besides, what if Nana says no to the idea and then Adam has a fit? I decide to wait.

This time when I reach Fred Carmel's I run around looking for the girl. I find her sitting in the ticket booth for the Ferris wheel. When she sees me she grins and calls, "Wait a minute, okay?"

"Okay," I call back, and I feel my heart quicken.

Six people are in line. When the girl has sold each of them a ticket she has a conversation with the man running the Ferris wheel, then takes off the apron she has been wearing, tosses it in the ticket booth, and hurries to my side.

"Hey," she says,

"Hi," I reply.

She nods back toward the Ferris wheel. "Do you want to ride?"

I shake my head. "I hardly have any money left."

"I see you here every day."

"This is the first carnival that's ever come to Millerton," I say. "I mean, that I can remember."

We are standing there, the two of us. We are both dressed in shorts and shirts and sandals. It is an extraordinarily hot day, and I can feel sweat forming at my temples, running down my face beside my braids. The girl, whose mass of dark hair falls almost to her waist, is fanning herself with a Fred Carmel poster.

"Do you work here?" I ask.

"My whole family does." She gestures over her shoulder. "My dad runs the Ferris wheel. My mom is with the sideshow."

"Really?" I say. What I am thinking is, Does she run it or is she in it? I don't know whether to be interested or horrified. I do not really want to find out that, for instance, her mother is John-Jane. On the other hand, if her mother *is* John-Jane, I might learn what lies beneath the half-and-half hair and the half-and-half clothing.

"Yeah," says the girl. "She's Pretzel Woman." She does not seem the least bit embarrassed by this.

I cannot think of anything to say except, "My name is

Hattie. What's yours?" And then I cringe because that sounds like something a talking doll might say.

But the girl just smiles and replies, "Leila Cahn." I guess when your mother is Pretzel Woman you can't be too judgmental about people. Briefly, I wish Nancy's mother were Pretzel Woman.

"So . . . do you . . ." I feel engulfed by awkwardness, which is the way I feel every time I have to give a talk in class, every time I am faced with a room full of Nana and Papa's company, every time I step into the ballroom of the Present Day Club for a party or a cotillion. I don't know what to do. I don't know what to say. What happens to my words? "Do you, um . . . ?"

Leila smiles at me again. "I know it's weird," she says.

"What?"

"To be a carnival kid."

"Why is it weird?" I know absolutely nothing about being a carnival kid.

"Well, I mean, to begin with, my mom is Pretzel Woman."

I look at Leila, and we begin to laugh.

"I guess you live around here," says Leila.

"Yes," I reply. We are standing under a huge leafy tree, but even so, we are sweating and Leila is fanning herself.

"Wait," says Leila. "Stay right here." She runs off. A few minutes later she returns with two large paper cups full of lemonade and ice. She hands me one.

"Thanks!" I say. "How much is it?" I'm not sure how much change is left in my pocket.

"It's free," Leila replies. "I got it from my uncle Fred."

"Uncle Fred? Fred Carmel?" I say. Leila nods. "Your uncle is Fred Carmel?" Leila nods again. "Wow." I'm impressed. Also, I have found my words. "So, what's it like to be a carnival kid?"

Leila tells me the most fascinating things. She and her family spend their lives traveling. In summertime the carnival goes from town to town in the northern states. In wintertime the carnival goes from town to town in the south and west, wherever the weather is warm enough. At the height of winter they usually spend a couple of months in Florida. Leila is twelve years old. She has a nine-year-old brother named Lamar. Leila and Lamar go to correspondence school, which Leila has to explain to me.

"We get our lessons in the mail," she says. "My parents help us with our assignments, and then we mail them back. We can work anytime we want, even in the summer, if we feel like it, and so I'm already starting eighth-grade assignments, and Lamar, he's starting fifth-grade."

"And you work here too? At the carnival?" I ask.

"We don't have to, but we like to. I think Lamar's helping my aunt Jacky at the Balloon Bust today."

"Is Aunt Jacky your uncle Fred's wife?"

"No. Uncle Fred is Mom's brother. Aunt Jacky is Dad's sister." Leila pauses. "This is a family business," she adds.

I have finished my lemonade and am swishing my straw around in the bits of ice that are left. "How long are you going to be in Millerton?" I ask.

Leila shrugs. "I'm not sure. I think until the middle of July, or maybe a little later."

Oh. I am disappointed. I was hoping Leila would say she was going to be here for months and months. Even though that would not make any sense. I look at my watch. "Uh-oh. I'd better go. I want to get home in time for lunch."

Leila's face falls.

"What?" I say.

"Nothing . . . well, it's just . . . are you going to come back?"

"Not today. But I can come tomorrow."

"Okay!"

On the walk home I think about Leila. A carnival kid. Who goes to correspondence school. And who doesn't seem to mind that I am shy. But then, Leila doesn't have a chance to make many friends, I realize. Maybe she's as surprised that I wanted to talk to her as I am that she wanted to talk to me.

On Friday I head for the carnival first thing in the morning. I find Leila near the front entrance, and I have the feeling she's waiting for me.

"Come on," she says, reaching for my hand. "Today I'm giving you the grand tour."

Well. Leila's grand tour is like going backstage at a theater. She introduces me to all her aunts and uncles and cousins. Also to Lamar and her mother and father. She takes me behind the counters of the games in the midway and of the concession stands for the food from many nations. I cannot believe it when I shake the hand of Pretzel Woman. Or when Leila and I go on some of the rides for free. Or when I see the trailer the Cahns live in.

"I told my parents I might stay here for lunch today," I tell Leila later that morning.

Leila beams. "Good! Let's go get hot dogs."

So we do. While we eat them Leila tells me about some of the places she's visited. I tell her about the boardinghouse and Miss Hagerty and Mr. Penny and Angel Valentine. And then I find myself telling her about Nana and Papa and finally Adam. "I don't even really understand what's wrong with him," I say.

Leila looks thoughtful. "I'd like to meet Adam one day," she replies.

And I realize that Adam still has not been to Fred Carmel's.

Eleven

O nce, when I was about four, I told Miss Hagerty that Millerton knows how to get dressed up. Miss Hagerty laughed and said, "You are absolutely right, Dearie."

It's true. Millerton does know how to get dressed up. And it gets dressed up for every holiday you can think of. Halloween and Christmas are my favorites. At Halloween, jack-o'-lanterns glow in the windows of the stores downtown. Orange lights are strung between the lampposts. And almost everybody decorates their yards with witches and ghosts, or sheaves of corn husks with gourds and ears of dried corn. At Christmas, the store windows are trimmed with holly and greens and red ribbons and candy canes. And the town is aglow. Entire houses are outlined in lights.

Independence Day may not be quite as spectacular as

Christmas, but it's still fun. Downtown Millerton turns red, white, and blue at the beginning of every July. American flags wave up and down Nassau Street, and in front of most houses. Kids twine red and blue crepe paper through the spokes of their bicycle wheels and ride around town in a purple blur.

The first thing I do on the morning of July 4th is peer out my window. I am hoping, hoping for blue sky and no clouds. My wish is granted. The sky looks like an azure mountain lake.

I run downstairs and fix Miss Hagerty's tray in a big hurry. When I set it on her bed I say, "No rain today. Not a cloud in sight."

Miss Hagerty grins. "Wonderful. We won't be rained out, then."

On the Fourth of July a band concert is held in the town square, and everyone brings picnics and talks and visits and eats while the Millerton Brass Band plays marches and show tunes and "My Country 'Tis of Thee" and "The Star-Spangled Banner." But last year the concert was rained out, and we sat at home and watched some fuzzy fireworks on the evening news. That is not going to happen this year.

I always go to the band concert with Mom and Dad and Nana and Papa. The band concert is one town event of which Nana approves. It is tasteful. The music is patriotic.

This year Adam will go with us. He seems to be very excited. "Wonderful, rousing, heart-lifting music, Hattie. Marches by Sousa. Oh, say can you see, broad stripes, bright stars, and Lucy dedicates a statue. Oh, ho, ho, ho, Hattie!"

Late in the afternoon, Mom and Dad and I leave our house carrying a large cooler. In it is a watermelon that Dad has fashioned into a basket by slicing off the top half except for the "handle," and scooping out the insides. He's filled it with pieces of fruit, making it an actual fruit basket. I think it is one of his more clever creations. Every year we offer to contribute something more to the picnic, but Nana likes to take control of things. What this means, basically, is that she likes to transport to the town square one of the spectacular meals that normally would be eaten in Nana and Papa's formal dining room. While everyone else at the picnic is eating hot dogs and potato salad on paper plates with plastic forks, we are eating hors d'oeuvres and steak and baby carrots on china plates with silverware.

I am aware that people stare at us. Even so, I wouldn't want to miss the concert.

Mom and Dad and I arrive at the town square and search the crowd for Nana and Papa and Adam. They should be easy to spot. Sure enough. They're sitting on a large blanket like everyone else, but the stack of gold-rimmed plates and the clanking of silver are hard to miss.

Adam looks up as we approach. "Hattie! Hattie!" he calls. "Dorothy! Jonathan! It's time for the annual fete. Look here! Sizzling barbecued chicken, a tantalizing array of vegetables —"

While Adam itemizes our meal, Dad unpacks the cooler. He sets the fruit basket carefully on a platter provided by Nana. Adam's eyes fall on it. For exactly one second he is speechless. Then a torrent of words pours forth. "Jonathan, how grand, how simply grand. A creation beyond all creations, yes, oh, yes!"

Adam is jumping up and down and wringing his hands. I glance around. Next to us a family with three boys has spread their picnic on a faded blue bedspread. On their plates are hot dogs and hamburgers and deviled eggs. They have been eating but have stopped with their hands halfway to their mouths to stare at Adam. They have actually stopped that way, like people in a cartoon.

I decide to stare back at one of them. I select the mother in the family, the person I hold responsible for teaching manners to her children. I grab a cookie from a plate, hold it halfway to my own mouth, and stare at her until she notices me. When she does, her face turns bright red and I feel gratified.

After he gets over the excitement of the watermelon basket, Adam settles down. We fill our plates with food and begin to eat as the band tunes up. Dad takes the movie camera out of its case and pans around the square. Then he focuses in on Mom, me, Nana, and Papa. Each of us waves and smiles. When he swings the camera around to Adam and says, "Smile!" Adam refuses to look at him. "Adam!" Dad calls. I know Adam hears him, but he begins to eat rapidly, shoveling in forkful after forkful of chicken. I don't know why he suddenly won't look at the camera. He just won't. Dad turns his attention back to the rest of us. Papa points to the chicken, then rubs his stomach in a grand circular motion. Mom mouths, "YUM, YUM, YUM." Still, Adam won't do anything but eat. I'm sitting next to him. I let out a long, low burp that I know only he can hear. Finally Adam laughs. Dad is happy, I am happy, everyone is happy.

The band finishes tuning up and begins playing something quiet that I don't recognize. Around me the crowd seems to ease into themselves. Voices grow softer. A few minutes later, when Jack parks the Good Humor truck at the edge of the square, there is no mad rush to it, like there is when it comes tinkling down our street on bright afternoons. Instead, here and there someone yawns and stretches, then stands slowly and searches for change before ambling to the truck to choose an ice-cream sandwich or a Popsicle.

I'm glad everyone is slowing down, keeping to themselves. The blankets become small islands that people are hesitant to step off of. I begin to relax.

"Well," says Nana as she and my mother stack our plates. "Who wants dessert?" She sounds very perky.

"Dessert," I repeat. "Yum. What is it?"

Nana reaches into one of her picnic baskets. "Strawberry and blueberry pie with whipped cream."

"Oh, red, white, and blue!" I exclaim. I glance at Adam, sure this will please him.

Adam's face looks hard, though. Hard and tight and actually a little frightening. "I want to get dessert from the Good Humor truck," he says.

"But Ermaline made —" Nana starts to say.

Adam jumps up. "I don't like strawberries! I want chocolate ice cream. I have enough money." He withdraws some change from his pocket. "And I want to see Sandy."

Papa frowns. "Sandy? Oh, Adam, Sandy doesn't drive the Good Humor truck anymore."

"Yeah, now it's Jack," I pipe up.

"I don't care who drives the damn truck," says Adam loudly. "I'm going to get ice cream." He begins loping through the crowd. Although he doesn't actually run over anyone's blanket, he pushes through groups of people and knocks over someone's lawn chair.

"Go with him, Hattie," says Nana, pushing me forward.

My heart is pounding, and my stomach feels sour, but when I catch up with Adam, he grins at me. "I have enough money for two ice creams," he says. "What do you want, Hattie? What do you want? Do you want a treat? Do you want ice cream? I scream, you scream, we all scream for ice cream!"

"I want —"

"Look! There's the truck! And there's the man. Is that man Jack, Hattie? Is he Jack?"

There is no line at the truck, and I am glad. "Yes, it's Jack," I say.

Jack sees me and calls, "Happy Fourth, Hattie!"

"Happy Fourth!" I reply. "Jack, this is my uncle Adam. Adam, this is —"

"Yes, yes, the famous Jack. Greetings, Jack. What do you have here in your splendid truck? I myself would like chocolate ice cream. Do you have chocolate ice cream for your royal subjects? And what would you like, Hattie? When Lucy was pregnant, she got cravings at four o'clock in the morning. She asked Ricky to bring her pistachio ice cream with hot fudge and sardines. Oh, boy, wonderful!"

Jack laughs gently. "Well, I don't have any sardines here."

Adam laughs too. He seems to calm down.

A moment later, Adam has his chocolate ice-cream bar and I have an ice-cream sandwich. We say good-bye to Jack and return to our blanket.

We have no sooner sat down than the quiet music becomes "When the Saints Go Marching In." The party mood returns to the crowd. People talk more loudly. I see the shadowy figures of men and women as they rise to talk with friends or to chase after children. Halfway through the song I realize that Adam is no longer on our blanket. I'm the only one who notices, since not only is it growing dark but six of Nana and Papa's friends have stopped to chat with them, and the grown-ups are busy getting coffee out of the silver urn.

I leap up. I have an idea where Adam is and, still licking the chocolate off of my fingers, I run to the bandstand.

Adam has placed himself directly behind the conductor and is dancing to the music. I have to admit that the music makes even me feel like dancing. But at Millerton's annual Fourth of July band concert, people do not dance. They sit and eat and talk and visit.

Only Adam dances. So of course he attracts a lot of attention. Quite a few people stop their eating and talking to turn and stare at the young man who is jumping up and down, up and down in time to the music. Sometimes he wrings his hands. Sometimes he calls out, "Happiness! Happiness!" which makes me smile. What a wonderful way to celebrate Independence Day.

The song ends, and another one begins. I glance over my shoulder. My parents and grandparents are still busy with their guests. I decide to wait until this new song ends and then try to talk to Adam. I don't think I should disturb him now.

I'm standing behind him, waiting, when I hear the words "freak show." I whirl around.

Well, there they are. Nancy and Janet. What a surprise. I shoot a look at them. And then, even though the music hasn't stopped, I take Adam by the arm and lead him toward our blanket. He allows this, just as he allowed me to walk him home on that early morning. As we make our way through the crowd he winds down, so that by the time we return to Nana and Papa he's just Adam again, talking about his chocolate ice cream.

I sit on the edge of the blanket, apart from everyone. My face is burning. Over the treetops I see fireworks showering the night sky. I think they are the fireworks at Fred Carmel's.

I am just sitting there, staring, when an absolutely horrible thought occurs to me. I don't know exactly what is wrong with Adam, but maybe it's one of those diseases that run in families. Maybe that's why Nana and Papa seem ashamed of him. And maybe . . . is that why Mom and Dad never told me about Adam? To keep the knowledge of his illness from me? Do they maybe even think that *I'm* a little like Adam? Is that why Mom wants me to be more like other kids — so she can prove to herself that I'm not going to turn out like Adam one day?

I twist around and look at my family. I can't stop the questions from coming. And I can't ask a single one of them.

Twelve

After July 4th my days fall into a pattern. In the mornings I fix Miss Hagerty's breakfast, eat my own breakfast with Mom and Dad and Mr. Penny, and check Angel Valentine's outfit and hairdo as she runs out the door. When I've taken care of all my chores, I head for the carnival, and Leila and I spend the entire rest of the day together, even lunchtime. Lunch is always hot dogs and lemonade, which Leila gets for free. Sometimes we run a booth or take tickets or call people to the sideshow. Sometimes we just try to find a cool, quiet place so we can sit and talk.

One day I say to Leila, "Doesn't it bother you that people pay money to stare at your mother? Doesn't it bother your mother?"

Leila frowns. "I don't know, I mean, if that's how they

want to spend their money. . . ." She trails off. "It's better than staring and *not* paying."

"I guess," I reply.

"Besides, it's just an act. Most of the performers in the sideshow are putting on an act, the ones who have learned how to do tricks or to wear special makeup and costumes. It's people like Chimp Boy and Baby Tess I worry about. People stare at them because of the way they were born. They say they don't mind, since how else are they going to earn a living? But, I don't know . . ."

"People stare at my uncle Adam," I tell her. "They call him a freak."

"You really like your uncle, though. I can tell."

"Yeah. I do. You know what I like best about him? I like how happy he can get. Most people don't get happy the way Adam does. When Adam is happy he jumps up and down like a little kid. Or he shouts, 'Happiness!'"

Leila grins. "Happiness," she repeats. She swallows the last of her hot dog bun. "Has he been here yet? I bet he would have fun."

He hasn't been to Fred Carmel's yet because of Nana's dim view of what she calls circus people, even though technically, Leila and her family are carnival people.

"I bet he would have fun too," I say.

"Then bring him," says Leila.

"I will."

When the time seems right.

The time seems right a few days later. It is Friday morning. I'm finishing up my chores, bringing in the broom from the front porch, when I see Adam come whistling up our walk.

"Happy July eighth, Hattie Owen!" he calls, waving vigorously.

"Hi, Adam!"

"Would Miss Angel Valentine be in residence?" he asks.

He is in an awfully good mood. But why can he never remember that Angel works? Maybe, I think, it's because Angel's job reminds him of the great differences between him and Angel. If Adam were a regular person, he'd probably be at work now too.

I decide not to point this out. Instead, I say, "Hey, Adam, would you like to go to the carnival with me?" Somehow walking with Adam all the way across town doesn't seem scary anymore, especially since Leila will be at the end of our journey, so I won't be on my own with Adam for long.

"To Fred Carmel's Funtime Carnival with the midway, prizes, sideshow, and food from many nations?"

"Yes."

"Right now?"

"Yes. Well, as soon as I've talked to Nana. But I think she'll say we can go."

Despite her feelings about circus people, Nana seems relieved by the thought of having Adam out of the house for an afternoon. And apparently she trusts us together. She knows I go to the carnival all the time. I get the feeling that Nana doesn't expect much from Adam except that he stay out of her hair and not embarrass her.

"Have fun!" Nana calls to us as we start down her front walk. Then, "Oh, Adam, wait. Wait right there." Nana disappears inside. When she returns she presses a ten-dollar bill into Adam's hand. "Treat yourself and Hattie to lunch and some games," she says.

I wait until we are out of Nana's hearing. "You won't be needing much of that money," I tell him. "We're going to get a free lunch. And we can go on rides for free too. We should pay for the games, though. I wouldn't feel right getting one of those giant prizes for free."

Adam is looking distracted. "Rides," he says.

"Yeah, for free. Lunch too."

"Really?"

"Yup. You haven't met my friend Leila yet."

Now I have Adam's attention.

"Leila? Who's Leila?"

I tell Adam about Leila and Lamar and the Cahns and their fascinating lives. By the time we reach the carnival, Adam is keyed up. The whirling rides, the smells of cotton candy and French fries, the music from the merry-go-round, and the crowds of people make him even more excited.

"Hattie, Hattie, my old friend, what a splendid place this is!" Adam has hurtled through the entrance to the carnival and is galloping from one attraction to the next. "A bundle of energy in Millerton's own backyard!" he cries. "Popcorn, peanuts, get yer red hots, red hots, right here. Lucy and Bob Hope and — oh, my, look skyward, Hattie, look skyward!"

I look up but I don't think I see whatever Adams sees up there. Just a speck of an airplane far away. I hope we can find Leila quickly. I hope I haven't made a mistake bringing Adam here.

The first place we look for Leila is at the ticket booth for the Ferris wheel, and thank goodness she's there. When she sees me, she raises her hand and waves. Then she spots Adam and jumps to her feet, pushing Lamar into her seat and saying, "Your turn!"

Leila unties her apron and runs out of the booth. "Hi, Hattie!" she says. "Is this Adam?"

Before I can answer, Adam, rocking back and forth on the balls of his feet, says, "Upon my word, Leila Cahn, niece of Fred Carmel himself, owner of the wonderful carnival. This is a holiday, a celebration, a reunion of the heavens! Glory, glory!"

"Hi," says Leila. She is smiling and I know she knows this is Adam. "How about a tour of the carnival? I gave Hattie one."

Leila doesn't wait for Adam to answer. She takes him by the hand, and suddenly we are in the world of the carnival. We start with the midway, where Adam uses some of Nana's money to play games. When he has lost four games in a row I see his body stiffen and his eyes fill with tears. "Not nice, not nice," he mutters.

"Let's make spin-art paintings," says Leila.

So we do. When Adam has evened out, I say to him, "Now how about a ride?"

"Any ride you want for free," adds Leila.

Adam drops his eyes. "Oh, no. No, thanks. Thank you very much, you are most kind, I am sure, but no rides, thank you."

"Really? How about the merry-go-round?" asks Leila. "Some of the horses don't even move up and down. Or you can just sit on a plain bench."

Adam is still looking at the ground. "Fred it's impossible to get seasick on a boat that is standing still tell that to my stomach."

For the first time, Leila looks confused. She glances at me.

"It's from *I Love Lucy*," I say. "I think he memorized all the shows."

Leila frowns. Then she says, "Do you get seasick, Adam? I mean, do you get motion sick on rides?"

"No."

Now we are stumped.

"But you don't want to go on any rides?" I ask.

"I like to watch the Ferris wheel," says Adam.

"Just watch it?"

"Yes."

So we stand outside the booth, where Lamar is taking tickets, and we watch the Ferris wheel turn slowly round and round above the carnival.

Finally Adam says, "I'm a little hungry, you know. My stomach is talking to me."

"Then let's get lunch," says Leila.

We sit at a table in the shade with our hot dogs and lemonade. Adam is still very quiet. He eats while Leila and I talk about books. Leila likes to read as much as I do, but she has never had a library card since her family never stays in one place for very long.

"How do you get books, then?" I ask her.

"We buy them at flea markets and rummage sales. And my aunt Dot always sends me books on my birthday."

"Hattie's birthday is coming up," says Adam.

"Oh, really? When?"

Adam comes to life. "On July sixteenth, Leila Cahn! July sixteenth. One week from tomorrow."

"Cool," says Leila. "I'll still be here. We can celebrate your birthday, Hattie."

Adam jumps up. "Leila, Leila! I have an idea. Come here."

Adam is not subtle.

I grin as I watch him pull Leila a little distance away from our table. He talks excitedly to her. His hands flap, and he begins to bounce up and down. And when they return a few minutes later, Adam is saying, "It's a mind trick, Leila, Leila, a mind trick, I tell you. A trick of the mind. Monday is the day you were born all right. Ask your parents. How about another date? Give me another date, a date of your choosing."

Leila obliges, smiling.

Later that afternoon I drop Adam off at Nana and Papa's.

"We ate hot dogs," Adam tells his mother, "and we watched the Ferris wheel but we didn't go on it, and we played games but we didn't win anything, and Leila is kind, kind, very kind. She goes to correspondence school. Oh, and a man didn't guess my weight, so I got this." Adam pulls a tiny jackknife out of his pocket.

Nana's smile fades. "Please give me that, Adam," she says. Adam hands it to her. "This is going to be one of those things you may keep but not touch. We'll put it in the case in the living room."

Adam stomps away from his mother.

Nana shakes her head. "I guess I don't expect you to know any better," she says to me. "And the circus people don't know Adam, of course, but still . . ."

Behind her, Adam sticks his tongue out at Nana as he starts up the stairs. And I turn my back on her and leave.

Thirteen

My days with Leila at the carnival are growing longer. One afternoon I am walking home so late that I see Angel Valentine coming home from work in the other direction. I look at my watch. Sure enough, it is after five o'clock.

Angel waves to me, bangle bracelets jingling. She is wearing a white lacy blouse so clean, it is almost sparkling, a red and orange and yellow striped skirt that falls in soft folds from her waist to below her knees, and a wide black leather belt. I think she looks a little like a gypsy or maybe a Spanish dancer.

I wave back, feeling very plain in my shorts and T-shirt and no jewelry of any kind. Even so, I run down the street to Angel so that we can walk back to our yard together. I don't get to spend much time alone with her.

"Where've you been?" Angel asks, dabbing at her damp temples with a hankie.

"The carnival," I reply.

Angel smiles. "The carnival. Wasn't that something?"

I know she is talking about the night the carnival opened.

"Did you have fun?" I ask. I am desperately hoping she will tell me something about the Frankie Avalon guy.

"We had a fine time."

"Did you go with . . ." I think I am blushing, but I have to ask anyway. "Is he your boyfriend?"

"Henry?"

"The guy with the convertible."

Angel smiles again, but this time the smile is more for herself. "Well, we haven't known each other long. But I suppose Henry is my boyfriend. We like each other very much."

"Is that what makes a boyfriend and a girlfriend? Liking each other very much?" I ask as we turn onto our walk.

"There's a little more to it than that, Hattie," says Angel, and then we both jump a mile when from behind a lilac bush a voice bellows, "Hattie! Hattie Owen! And the lovely Miss Angel Valentine! A great good evening to you both!"

"Adam!" I let out a gasp.

Where did he come from? I think he has been waiting for us, and this sudden appearance has made my heart pound.

Adam stands just a little too close to Angel and me as he says, "The gods are smiling down upon us on this heavenly summer's eve, smiling down like great Cheshire cats, Cheshire cats in the sky. Hattie and Angel, Cheshire cats in the sky."

I take a step back and notice that Angel is backing up too. There is something about Adam's grin, something about the way he has narrowed his eyes just slightly, that looks all wrong. Then Adam turns, runs to the porch, crashes down into a chair, and sits, leaning forward, rubbing his hands together. Angel and I follow him. Gingerly we sit on the porch swing. In seconds Adam transforms himself. He melts into the back of the chair, his breath coming more evenly, and says, "Angel Valentine, you look like a summer garden this evening."

"Why, thank you," Angel replies. "This is a new skirt."

"It's very becoming," says Adam primly.

I see that his eyes have slipped down from Angel's face and have landed on her chest again.

Maybe it's because of this, maybe not, but Angel stands up suddenly, which joggles the swing, and says, "I'd love to sit out here and chat with you, but I have a date tonight."

I almost say, "With Henry?" but I do not think Adam is going to want to hear about Angel's boyfriend. I cringe, waiting for an explosion, for Adam to stomp off the porch, to shout, for the tears to come. Instead, he looks interested and says, "A date! A date on a Monday night. Very cosmopolitan, Angel Valentine. Very chic!"

Which is exactly what I am thinking.

Angel smiles charmingly. "We're going to a French restaurant," she adds.

The nearest French restaurant is all the way over in Sargentsville. This must be some date.

Adam says, "Lucy ate snails in a French restaurant and she didn't like them one bit. Don't eat any snails at the French restaurant, Angel Valentine."

Angel smiles and promises not to. Then she glides inside.

I watch Adam. For once he is not watching Angel. The moment she has disappeared up the stairs, Adam jumps to his feet, stands stiffly in front of me with his hands behind his back.

"Hattie Owen, my old friend," he says, and he sounds as if he is going to give a speech he has memorized. "As you know, your birthday is coming up." He pauses.

I guess I am supposed to say something. I nod. "On Saturday."

"And Leila Cahn and I would like to do something special for you. You must have a birthday party. You absotively must. Everyone has enough friends for a birthday party. Because, you see, you only need one friend for a party. One is enough. Two is enough. Anything is enough." Adam pulls a folded piece of paper out of his pocket and hands it to me.

I open it. Big crawly handwriting swims across the page.

"Read it, Hattie!" cries Adam. "Read it out loud."

I clear my throat. "'You are invited to a party,'" I begin. "'Date: Friday, July fifteenth. Place: Fred Carmel's Funtime

Carnival. Time: starting at three-thirty P.M. in the afternoon on the dot. Occasion: Hattie Owen's twelfth birthday. Given by: her friends Adam and Leila.'"

I lower the paper. "Wow, Adam. This is great."

"You can come, can't you?" says Adam. He is wringing his hands, and his eyes are begging me to say yes.

But I am thinking that Nana's cotillion is on Friday afternoon, and I actually don't know whether this is a problem. I don't want to disappoint Adam. And I certainly don't want to go to the cotillion. But Nana . . .

Adam is staring at me intensely, the way you would stare in a staring game. He's still standing, and he has placed his hands on his knees and is leaning into me, his face just inches from mine. Searching for my answer, I guess. How can I say no to him?

How can I say no to Nana?

I want to run inside and ask someone for advice. My parents are always busy with supper at this hour. But Miss Hagerty will be in her room.

"Just a sec," I say to Adam.

I am halfway through the door when Adam grabs the back of my shirt and pulls. "What are you doing?" he says.

I fall into him. "I'm —"

"Don't you want to come to our party?"

I look at my watch, look through the screen door, look at

Adam's face. "Let me walk you home," I say. "I want to show your invitation to Nana. It's beautiful. And it's the first invitation I ever received to my own birthday party."

This makes Adam smile.

We set off down the street. Adam is all uneven today, and I am a little afraid. He makes a lot of noise as we walk along. He jingles the change in his pocket and he hums under his breath. Sometimes he stops humming in order to puff his cheeks full of air, then pop them with his index fingers. I begin to think that the best I can hope for when we reach Nancy's and Janet's will be humming and jingling without cheek-popping. But we walk by their houses without seeing them.

Adam and I turn the corner onto his street, and I can see Nana standing on the front steps of the house. She waves to us, trying to look gay and pleased, but I know she has been feeling worried. She has probably called Mom and Dad, who have said they haven't seen Adam or me all day long.

"Hi, Nana!" I call. "Look at this."

I'm sure Nana wants to say something to Adam, but I am waving the invitation over my head. She frowns at him as she takes the piece of paper from me. "What is it?" she asks.

"Adam just brought it over," I tell her. "He and Leila are giving me a birthday party."

Nana reads the paper. Her frown is not going away. "Leila is the circus —?"

"Leila is Leila Cahn, whose family owns Fred Carmel's,"
I say. "She's my new friend."

"And Hattie is going to have a birthday party this year,"
adds Adam. "We are going to give her one."

"Hattie has a birthday party every year," says Nana.

"With grown-ups," says Adam. "Not with her friends." I
see a muscle move on the side of his face, and I think he is
clenching his jaw.

"Well, Adam, this is a very nice gesture," Nana says finally. "But Friday is the cotillion and —"

"But Hattie doesn't —" Adam starts to say, and for one
horrible instant I think that somehow he knows how I feel
about the cotillion and is going to tell Nana I don't want to go.
"Hattie doesn't want to miss her own birthday party," he says.

"Couldn't you have the party on the weekend?" asks
Nana sensibly. "After all, Hattie's birthday is on Saturday."

"No, it has to be on Friday!" Adam is shouting suddenly.
"Leila has to work on Saturday. It's the busiest day."

Saturday may be the busiest day at Fred Carmel's, but I
doubt that Leila *has* to work.

"Adam," says Nana, and she has made her voice very
quiet. She holds out her hand to him, and he swats it
away. "How about Friday evening, then? Or sometime on
Sunday?" She takes a step backward, bumps into one of the
porch columns, and steadies herself.

"No! I can't just change our plans. Our plans are important, they're important, I'm important. We made plans. Why aren't my plans important?"

"Adam, your plans are important," I say. "I want to go to the party. I do." I look at Nana. She is still holding on to the column.

"But Adam, Friday —" says Nana.

I see the red that is creeping up Adam's face. Adam opens his mouth like he is yawning. No, like he is about to scream, to let out a bloodcurdling movie-monster scream. I put my hands over my ears, waiting. But then Adam closes his mouth, and his face crumples. He bursts into tears. He cries in the loud way a little child might. Betsy said to me once that she wished it were still okay for her to cry like that — to screw up her face, draw in a huge breath, and just let out a wail every time she felt frustrated. And that is what Adam is doing now.

After a few moments his wails subside, and he sinks down on the porch steps and sobs quietly.

"Nana?" I say.

Nana can't answer me at first. She is about to cry herself, I can tell. She takes a step toward Adam's back as if she might touch his shoulder. Then she draws away, says, "Of course you can go to Adam's party on Friday, Hattie," turns, and walks into the house.

I watch Adam. "Thank you for the party," I say. "I can't wait."

Adam doesn't answer.

I sit down next to him. I don't know if it's okay to put my arm around him, so instead I inch closer and closer until our shoulders are touching. Adam buries his head in his hands, then turns and leans in to me. At last I know it is okay to touch him, and I wrap both of my arms around him.

"No one knows," says Adam, "what it is like."

"No," I reply, although I think I might know more than most people.

"You are not an alien, Hattie. I am the only true alien."

But Adam is wrong. I am a true alien too.

Fourteen

Today is Friday, and it is the last day I will be eleven years old.

Mom and I have been invited to lunch with Nana. We do this sometimes, have Girls' Lunches. Only today Adam will be there too. I don't mind going to Nana's for a Girls' Lunch nearly as much as I mind having Nana to lunch at our house. When Nana gives a Girls' Lunch she is in control, and when Nana is in control, she's happy.

At a Girls' Lunch we eat in Nana's dining room, and Ermaline serves us teeny sandwiches with no crust on the bread, and little individual plates of fruit and cheese, and then we have tea and cookies for dessert. Ermaline stays in the kitchen unless Nana calls her by stepping on the hidden buzzer. I would dearly love to press that buzzer, but it is strictly forbidden for anyone except Nana to press it. Mom says it has always been that way. Nana is the queen.

Mom fusses and fumes before every single Girls' Lunch. She says what a pain it is to have to take off her work clothes in the middle of the day, but I notice that she spends practically forever in front of the mirror, adjusting her clothes and jewelry, dabbing perfume behind her ears. She is not doing this just to please Nana. I think that secretly she loves an excuse, any excuse, to be Nana's princess.

Later, as Mom and I walk along Grant Street, Mom says, "You look lovely, Hattie." Her earlier grumbling about the Girls' Lunch is over. "I can't believe you're almost twelve years old. Just think. This time twelve years ago, nineteen forty-eight, they said a hurricane was coming, but instead you arrived."

I smile. Then I say, "Mom? How come you and Dad never had any other kids?"

"My goodness," says Mom. "Where did that question come from?"

I shrug.

"Well . . ." Mom's smile has faded. She clears her throat. "I don't know. I guess it was just that you came along and you were perfect. So we decided to quit while we were ahead."

It is on the tip of my tongue to say, "You mean to quit before you had a kid like Adam?" but the words will not come.

I think I have ruined something, because Mom and I walk the rest of the way in absolute silence. I hope that Ermaline and the no-crust sandwiches and tea and cookies will restore Mom's mood.

Adam greets us at Nana's, wearing a suit and tie.

"Welcome, welcome, Hattie and Dorothy!" he exclaims. "Dorothy, go right on in." He gives Mom a little shove through the front door, then grabs my wrist and whispers to me, "It's a good thing your party is this afternoon, Hattie. Ermaline fixed ladies' food, which wouldn't fill a canary, wouldn't fill half a canary, wouldn't fill a full canary. But don't worry because we can eat at Fred Carmel's. Leila and I have everything planned, don't you worry, don't you worry for one second."

I am not worried, but I whisper thank you to Adam, and we head inside. My stomach flutters when I see Nana. She is wearing a much fancier outfit than she would ordinarily wear to a Girls' Lunch, which means that she is already dressed to be a chaperone at the cotillion. She eyes my own nice but definitely not cotilliony dress, but says nothing. Instead, she ushers us into the dining room. The enormous table is set for four — Nana at the end, Adam to her right, Mom to her left, and me next to Mom. More than half the table is empty.

We have no sooner sat down than Nana says, "Well, Hattie, I hope you are going to enjoy your birthday party this afternoon." Adam and I glance at each other. "It sounds like fun," she continues. No part of her is smiling. "All right. If we're ready to eat, I'll ring Ermaline."

I see Adam lunge to his left then, and I know exactly what he has done. He has done what I have wanted to do my whole life. He has stepped on Nana's buzzer.

"Adam!" says Nana.

I see Adam lunge three more times, which explains why Ermaline comes flying into the dining room, looking alarmed. "Ma'am?" she says to Nana.

"Ermaline, I'm sorry. That was an accident."

Ermaline hesitates. "Are you ready to be served?"

Nana casts a glance at Adam. "I'm not sure Adam is. Adam, are you going to be able to eat with us in the dining room, or do you need to eat in the kitchen?"

Adam's face reddens. I think my face is reddening too. I know how tempting that buzzer is.

Adam faces Nana. "Are you going to be able to eat with us in the dining room, or do you need to eat in the kitchen?" he says.

"Adam," says Nana.

"Adam," says Adam.

"Not one more word."

"Not one more word."

Nana is old. And she is little. I bet I weigh more than she

does. But she has a loud voice. Nana stands up now and uses it. She glares at Adam, then points at the door to the dining room. "Out!" she says, as if Adam is a dog. "Out!"

"Mother —" says Mom, but I don't find out what she was going to say, because Nana silences her with a single sidelong glance.

Adam is out the door in two seconds, and I know better than to leave the table and go after him. I don't see him again until lunch is over. Mom and Nana are chatting in the foyer, and I go looking for Adam and find him in the sitting room.

At first he won't talk to me.

"Did you eat anything?" I ask him.

Adam has turned one of the armchairs so that it faces outside, and he is staring into the garden.

"Did Ermaline give you lunch?" I say.

Nothing.

"We can have the party another day," I say finally.

Adam is silent for so long that I think he is not going to answer me. I am pretty sure we won't have the party after all, and I am starting to wonder if now I will have to go to the cotillion, when Adam says, "The party is still on, Hattie. Come back at three-fifteen." The way he says this, it is the first time I have felt that Adam is actually older than I am, and I remember that he is my uncle, and not just my friend.

"Okay," I say.

I don't know what to expect when I go back to Nana's at three-fifteen. For all I know, Adam is being punished, and Nana will grab me, send me home to change, and make me go to the cotillion with her.

But Adam greets me at the door and, as Cookie would say, he looks fresh as a daisy. Fresh as a very strange daisy, though. He has taken a shower and washed his hair, which is now carefully parted along the middle, and all greased down. He is wearing plaid shorts, a tailored white shirt with every single button buttoned, and a red and green bow tie. Also, he is wearing loafers without socks.

"Hattie, Hattie, Hattie, my old friend. Hattie, the birthday girl. Girl who can lift the corners of our universe, girl who is a sight for sore eyes, girl who is eleven almost twelve years old, girl who is about to have her first birthday party with friends, girl —"

"Adam!" I hear Nana call.

"Good-*bye!*" shouts Adam, and slams the door behind him. "We're off," he says to me.

Adam is clutching a brown paper bag. He takes my hand and heads for the carnival at a pace so brisk, I have to run to keep up with him. I feel like a kid holding her father's hand and trying to match the stride of his long legs. Adam whistles the theme from *I Love Lucy* as we hurry along.

Eventually, he begins to sing. "I love Lucy and she loves me. We're as happy as two can be!"

I am out of breath by the time we reach Fred Carmel's. I look at my watch. Right on time. And Leila is waiting for us at the main entrance.

"Happy birthday, Hattie!" she calls.

"It isn't her birthday, not really, you know," says Adam. "Not until tomorrow, the sixteenth, Saturday, the sixteenth of July, although Hattie was born on a Friday."

"Well, happy birthday a little early then," says Leila.

"Let the birthday fun begin!" cries Adam.

"Yeah, it's your special day, Hattie," says Leila. "Anything you want all afternoon is free — rides, food, games, anything."

"Wow," I say. I've gotten free stuff at the carnival before, but I try to keep it under control.

"What do you want to do first, Hattie Owen?" asks Adam, who is jumping up and down.

"Rides," I say. "Rides first."

Adam lands on the ground and stays there. "Rides," he repeats, and he lets out his breath. "All right."

I know rides are not Adam's favorite thing, but I just have to go on a few this afternoon. This is too good to miss.

Leila and I start with the merry-go-round. Adam sits on a bench and watches us. Then we head for the Tilt-A-Whirl, which nearly makes me sick but is still exciting. Adam sits on another bench. When Leila and I climb into a car on the Ferris wheel, Adam stands below us, just behind the ticket booth, and watches. From high above him I can see his head slowly following our progress, around and around.

"Now what?" says Leila when we step out of our car a few minutes later.

"Could we get ice cream?" I ask her. I don't want to take advantage.

"Sure, sure," Adam answers. "Ice cream all around, I scream you scream, we all scream for ice cream! . . . Leila, Leila, come here."

Adam whispers something in Leila's ear, and Leila nods her head. "Okay," she says. "Get the ice cream and go sit over there. I'll be right back."

When Adam and I have gotten three cups of vanilla ice cream, we sit at a picnic table.

"What are we waiting for?" I ask Adam.

"You'll see," he says. And the next thing I know, he is singing, "Happy birthday to you, happy birthday to you!"

His voice is joined by Leila's, and she appears carrying a small cake with four candles, their flames trailing to the side in the hot breeze.

"Happy birthday, dear Hattie!" sing Adam and Leila. "Happy birthday to you!"

Leila has made the cake herself. She says it is her birthday present to me. Then Adam hands me the paper bag. "And this is mine," he says.

I open the bag and pull out a tiny wooden box.

"*I* made *that* myself," says Adam.

"Really?" The box is exquisite. On the lid is a round knob. I lift it and look inside. Polished wood. Smooth.

"You can put it in your pocket and keep your loose change in it," says Adam. "I made it at my school, my old school, I won't be going back there, you know."

"Adam, it's beautiful," I say. I want to hug him, but Adam is in a state of high excitement, jiggling and bouncing in his seat. So I reach across the table and hold his hand.

The rest of the party is perfect. We eat candy apples and then play games, and Adam finally wins a stuffed animal prize. He chooses a small blue tiger, and it makes him so happy that he jumps up and down in ecstasy, wringing his hands and singing, "I am Lily of the Valley! I am Lily of the Valley!" which I suspect is from a Lucy show. Later, he loses the tiger but doesn't care at all. He just wanted to win it in the first place.

When we are walking home, I tell Adam this was the best birthday party I ever had.

"I love Lucy and she loves me!" sings Adam.

The wooden box is in my pocket, and I think how nice it will be always to have a reminder of Adam with me.

Fifteen

On my birthday, my real birthday, the day I turn twelve at 2:22 in the afternoon, Mom and Dad give me another party. It is the same one we have every year. The guests are always Mom, Dad, Nana, Papa, Cookie, and our boarders. This year Adam is a guest too.

"Do you have the box, the little wooden box, your birthday present, Hattie?" Adam is pushing through our front door ahead of Nana and Papa, who are each carrying a shopping bag full of presents. "Everyone else is giving you their presents today," he says, "but I already gave you yours. You liked it, didn't you, Hattie, you liked your present? Ethel didn't like Lucy's at all. Well Ethel I — I think they're kinda cute what are they well they're hostess pants you wear 'em when you give smart dinner parties oh I was wondering what to wear to all those smart dinner parties I give."

"I love the box," I assure Adam. "It's right here in my pocket, see?" I pull it out and show him, shake it so he can hear that it really is full of my loose change.

Dad films the party, of course. Films me opening my presents, films everyone seated around the dining room table wearing goofy hats, films me cutting the cake, films Adam sticking his finger in the icing and swiping off the largest pink rose for himself. Luckily there is no sound to go with Dad's movies or we would be able to hear Nana's cry of displeasure as Adam slurps up the rose and reaches out for another one with the same sticky finger he just licked. The camera stops then, and Papa tells Adam he will have to go sit in the car.

"No, please, let him stay," I say. "I don't mind about the cake."

"Well, I do," says Nana. "Adam knows better."

"But I want him to stay. It's my party."

Adam doesn't hear this, though. He has already slammed out the front door and is stomping toward home.

Dad sets the camera down. The dining room is silent. Miss Hagerty and Mr. Penny are looking at their plates. Cookie examines a crumb on her fork. Angel Valentine jumps up and says she has an errand to run downtown. So the party ends.

Nana and Papa head for home. Most likely, they will find Adam along the way. I'm worried about his mood, but no one else mentions him. Mom says, "Hattie, it's your birthday. No chores, no cleaning up, and you don't need to help with dinner tonight. Go do whatever you want to do for the rest of the afternoon."

What I want to do is read, so I take the pile of new books I have been given and sit on the front porch with them until Cookie calls me in to dinner.

The invitations to Nana and Papa's dinner party are printed on cream-colored cards edged in gold, each protected by a small sheet of tissue paper. I have traced my finger over the raised letters many times since Mom and Dad's invitation arrived. The party is to be held in one week, on the Saturday after my birthday. The invitation has been tacked to the bulletin board in the kitchen for days now, and I can't help feeling that Nana probably didn't intend for something so fancy to wind up with a hole in it, stuck next to a batch of Green Stamps and supermarket coupons.

Nana and Papa give a very fancy dinner party twice each year, once at Christmas and once during the summer. I have wondered if this summer's might be postponed until a new school is found for Adam and he is out of the house. But I guess not. I'm pretty sure, though, that Adam will not be attending the dinner. For one thing, children are never invited to the summer party. I know Adam is not exactly a child, but he is sort of a child. And anyway, Nana likes her parties to be perfect. She will not want someone walking around sticking his fingers in the hors d'oeuvres and reciting lines from *I Love Lucy.*

What this means is that Adam and I will be on our own on Saturday night. Adam will probably have to spend the evening in his room. And I could spend it in mine, reading my new books. Or I could visit with Miss Hagerty, but she wants to teach me to needlepoint, and I'm not interested. I could also, I think, go to the carnival. I haven't been to the carnival at night since I went with Mom and Dad. Leila and I could ride the lit-up rides together, and sit at a darkened picnic table eating ice cream while the moon rises.

I wonder if I would be allowed to go.

One night when we are watching the news on TV, I say, "On Saturday when you go to Nana and Papa's party, could I go to the carnival?"

"At night without us?" says Mom. "I don't know . . ."

"I would be with Leila," I say. "I would spend the whole evening with her."

Mom and Dad look at each other.

"Leila's parents are always around," I add.

"I guess it would be all right," says Mom.

"As long as you wait for me to pick you up after the party," says Dad. "I don't want you walking home by your-self in the dark."

"I'll wait for you," I say.

The next day I tell Leila about my plan, and she says, "What about Adam? Can he come too?"

It's true that Adam will be stuck in his room, but I'm pretty sure he will not be allowed to go to the carnival at night without Nana and Papa.

"I don't think so," I tell Leila.

Later, after all that happens with Adam that night and in the days following, I am never quite sure what made me suggest to Adam that he sneak out of his house and go to the carnival with me. Maybe it doesn't matter. Somehow the idea comes up, and Leila and I talk and talk about it, knowing it is wrong but lured by its daring.

"It doesn't seem right that Nana and Papa should make him stay in his room during the party," I say.

"Like they're hiding him away," says Leila.

"He'd have a lot more fun at the carnival," I add. "And he's never seen it at night."

"Maybe you could tell him to sneak out of his house after the party starts."

"Maybe."

"But then what would you do with Adam when your father comes to pick you up?"

This is a good question. "I could tell him that Adam came to the carnival on his own, that we just ran into him after I got here."

Leila looks doubtful.

In the end, I decide that probably there is no way to do this without getting into some sort of trouble, and that is a risk I'm willing to take. I want Adam to have one wild, thrilling evening with no one around to tell him to use his party manners. One evening without Nana hovering around trying to make him perfect.

Soon enough Leila will be gone and Adam will go off to a new school, and the three of us will never have this chance again.

On Friday, the day before Nana and Papa's party, I tell Adam about our idea.

"Oh, oh, what an adventure, Hattie Owen! An adventure indeed. Better than when Lucy goes to Hollywood. Better than when she goes to Europe or Florida. More like her Martian adventure with Ethel! Count me in, count me in, Hattie, I will be there with bells on."

"But you have to remember not to mention this to Nana or Papa," I say.

"They are evil, evil people," Adam replies darkly.

"Meet me on the corner tomorrow night at seven-thirty," I say. "And remember not to let anyone see you leave the house."

"Righto, bingo, over and out," replies Adam.

*　　*　　*

The next night Adam is waiting for me when I reach the corner. "Hattie! Hattie!" He is jumping up and down. "I did it, I escaped and no one saw me. I am out of the loony bin on a free pass! Let the fun begin!"

I hurry us down the street, afraid someone will see us. Adam is boinging around, jumping, humming, singing. "I love Lucy and she loves me!"

We arrive at Fred Carmel's just as the lights are being turned on. From the parking lot we watch as darkened shapes come to life.

"Magic," whispers Adam as the Tilt-A-Whirl suddenly appears in the distance, then the Ferris wheel.

We walk to the entrance, where Leila is waiting for us. Behind her is the merry-go-round, a golden glow that lights her hair. Adam is right. Leila looks magic, the merry-go-round looks magic, we are surrounded by magic on this forbidden adventure.

Now Adam, overwhelmed, can barely speak. He watches the merry-go-round for two complete turns, then looks to his left and watches the Ferris wheel. Around and around goes his head.

"It's too good," he whispers at last.

"What? The Ferris wheel?" Leila says.

"Yes." Adam is still whispering. "Let's ride it."

"Really? You want to go on the Ferris wheel?" I say. "Are you sure?"

Adam nods.

"Okay," reply Leila and I at the same time.

Lamar is in the ticket booth, and he waves to us as we join the end of the line. Slowly we make our way forward and climb the four wooden steps up to the ride. Mr. Cahn is at the top of the steps and he helps us into one of the cars.

"I'll sit next to Adam," I say.

Mr. Cahn buckles us in, checks the buckles, then checks them again. "Okay," he says, "you're all set."

He lowers a bar over Adam and me, lowers the other one over Leila. Adam grips our bar tightly. His knuckles turn white.

Leila looks at his hands, looks at me, looks back at Adam. "Are you sure you want to go?" she asks him. "My dad could let us out right now."

Adam shakes his head. I'm actually not sure what that means. He doesn't want to go? He doesn't want to be let out? But it doesn't matter because suddenly our car jerks forward and we are lifted up. We rise above the carnival, the lights falling away beneath us.

"Oh, ho, ho, ho!" cries Adam.

Someone from the car just below us turns around to look up at Adam, and I stick my tongue out at her.

We reach the very top of the ride, and spreading away from us wherever we look are the lights of Millerton. We are the sun and there is our universe, I am thinking, just as

Adam says softly, "It's Neverland, it's Oz, it's Nirvana. Oh, it's the center of the universe." He tips his head back to look up at the stars.

Our car glides down toward the ground, then rises, glides to the ground, rises once more. We are at the top of the Ferris wheel for the third time when I hear a great screech of metal and we grind to a halt, our seats rocking.

"What's wrong?" I ask Leila.

"It must be stuck. That happens sometimes. My dad always fixes it."

I glance at Adam.

"We're lucky!" Leila goes on. "We're stuck at the *very* top. It's the best place to be stuck. You can look at the view all you want."

"I think I see Grant Av —"

"Oh, ho, ho, ho!"

"Adam?" I say, because this is not a happy shout.

"Oh, ho, ho, ho, *oh, ho, ho, ho,* OH, HO, HO, HO." His voice rises with each syllable, and when he shrieks out the last "ho" he bangs his hands on the bar.

The woman in the car below turns around to stare at Adam again, and someone from another car calls, "Shut up, jerk."

"Adam," says Leila, "I told you — my dad will fix this. It happens all the time."

Adam doesn't hear her. He shrieks and shrieks and shrieks. No words, just terrified sounds. My hands begin to shake. I remember when I comforted Adam on his front porch, but I know better than to touch him now.

I want to slide under the bar and crawl next to Leila. I am afraid of the stranger next to me.

Sixteen

Adam," says Leila, "my dad will fix the Ferris wheel." She speaks very slowly and very clearly.

Adam throws his head back and howls. "Do it now!"

"It takes time," Leila tells him.

"Somebody shut up that werewolf," yells the man who has already called Adam a jerk.

"*You* shut up, you —" I start to say, but Leila reaches across the car and puts her hand on my wrist.

"Don't say anything to him," she whispers loudly.

I'm not even sure what I was going to call the man, but I don't finish the sentence.

"Fix the damn car! Fix the damn car! Oh, ho, *ho,* HO!"

I turn in my seat so that I am sitting sideways. "Adam," I say, facing him now. He won't look at me. "Adam." He is banging on the bar. "Adam." Bang, bang, bang.

I reach out; I don't know how else to get his attention. And he knocks my arm away with such force that I am thrown backward against the side of the car. My shoulder burns. "Adam!" I shout.

"Don't touch me, you little . . ." Adam's last words are lost in a hail of activity. He is rocking back and forth, back and forth, and our car is pitching with him. At the same time he's trying to wrench the bar over our heads, and he is so strong — I can see his arm muscles straining — that he might be able to do it.

Leila leans out of the car and peers over the edge. "Dad! Dad!" she shouts.

"We're working as fast as we can!" Mr. Cahn shouts back to her.

"But Dad, he's —"

And at this moment, with a grinding shriek of metal, Adam succeeds in forcing the bar up over our heads. Then he is on his feet.

Leila and I lunge forward. "Adam, *sit down!*" Leila commands.

"Shut up, shut up, shut up!" Adam shrieks, but he sits down.

I look at the cars above and below us. The man who called Adam names is shouting instructions to someone on the ground. And the staring woman is still staring, but now she's staring at Leila and me, not at Adam, and she looks concerned. "Stay calm, girls," she says. "You're doing a good job. Just stay calm."

I barely hear her. Adam has stood up again and has swung his leg over the side of our car.

I begin to scream.

At the same time the woman yells, "Get back in the car!"

And the man yells, "Call the police! Somebody call the police!"

"They're on their way," I hear Mr. Cahn say from below.

The police, oh Lord, the police.

I don't care what Adam might do to me, but he cannot, simply cannot, climb out of our car. We are . . . how high up? Two stories? Three? More?

"Leila, help me," I say. "Grab his arms."

Leila and I grab Adam's arms and yank him backward. The three of us fall to the floor of the car.

"Get off! Get off!" Adam flails at us, with his hands, his feet. He hits, he kicks, then he scrambles to his knees and finally stands on one of the seats.

The look on his face, I think, is of pure terror. And I remember the time, a year or so ago, when I scared my father with an old Halloween mask. I had just meant to startle him, to make him laugh. Instead, I truly frightened him, and I will never, ever forget the look on his face. It was the kind of terrified look that reminds you that no matter how rational or grown up a person might seem, some part of him is absolutely sure — *knows* — that an evil other-world exists just outside of our regular, everyday world. And that although we don't expect that world to collide with our calm, predictable one . . . well, really, at any moment that is exactly what might happen.

I look at Adam now and see that he is terrified, terrified, terrified. How often has he felt like this?

"The police are on their way," I hear Mr. Cahn call.

And then someone screams, two people, three.

"Hattie!" Leila shouts. "Get *up*."

I scramble to my feet. Adam, only one foot left in our car now, is edging his way along the lighted bars of metal that make up the Ferris wheel.

"Grab him!" shouts the woman.

And just as Leila and I reach for him, the Ferris wheel jerks forward.

"Adam, it's fixed!" says Leila.

"Come back!" I say.

I hear the wail of a distant siren.

Adam won't come back into the car, though, and as the Ferris wheel begins its descent, Leila and I can do nothing but grab his ankle and hold on tight. We hold on all the way down, and I think that Mr. Cahn is making the Ferris wheel move faster than usual.

Adam kicks at us, trying to shake us off. He kicks so hard, my teeth rattle, but I will not let go.

At the bottom, the Ferris wheel jerks to another stop. Leila and I are still struggling to our feet when two police officers grab Adam, pry him off the metal bars, and pull him to the ground, where they try to put a pair of handcuffs on him.

"Stop!" I say. "Don't hurt him!" Leila and I fly after them. "Leave him alone. He's not going to hurt you."

But I am not sure about that. Adam is shouting, "Oh, ho, ho, ho!" and fighting the officers, twisting and kicking and biting. They struggle to fasten the handcuffs around his wrists.

"Are you okay?" Mr. Cahn has appeared, and he puts one arm around Leila and the other around me.

"We're okay," Leila says, even though we are scraped and bruised and some of our clothing is torn.

A huge crowd has gathered. It started to gather while we were stuck on the Ferris wheel, and now it is even larger, everyone staring at Adam, staring at the policemen. No one says much, but I can read in their eyes what they think of Adam. They are all glad he's not related to them, that somebody else has to deal with him.

Mrs. Cahn manages to push through the crowd and she joins us, giving me a hug. "It's going to be all right, Hattie," she says.

I want to turn my face to her shoulder and melt into her, forget about Adam. But I can't stop watching him.

"Hattie! Hattie!" Two more figures push through the crowd. Dad and Papa.

"What's going on?" Dad cries, and he looks scared.

Papa approaches the policemen. "Hey!" he says.

He puts a hand out to Adam, but one of the officers blocks his way. "I'm sorry, Mr. Mercer."

"What's going on?" Dad says to me.

"We were on the Ferris wheel and it got stuck and Adam just . . . he kind of went crazy."

"But what is Adam doing here at the carnival?"

"He came with me —" I start to say.

I stop talking because one of the policemen finally manages to close the handcuffs around Adam's wrists. They clasp his arms and start to walk him through the crowd.

"Stand back!" they say, and the people slowly part, their eyes never leaving Adam.

"Where are you taking him?" calls Papa. He's running after them, running after them wearing his tuxedo and his black dress shoes, which are now all dusty.

"To the hospital," one replies.

"Is that really necessary?"

Dad has grabbed me by the elbow and is dragging me after Adam and Papa and the officers. I look over my shoulder, look for Leila, but I can't find her in the crowd.

"Hattie," says Dad harshly, "come *on*."

The officers have not answered Papa's question. Obviously it is necessary to take Adam to the hospital, because he has still not stopped struggling. Even when the policemen lift him off the ground and try to carry him along by his arms, he kicks and flails.

I am not very surprised when I see an ambulance drive through the entrance to Fred Carmel's. The police officers drag Adam to it, and in about one second a straitjacket has been fastened around him and he has been loaded inside. Papa climbs in beside him. "We're going to St. Mary's," he calls to us before the doors bang shut and the ambulance turns around and heads off. It drives silently, but in a big hurry.

I look at Dad. He begins to talk a mile a minute. "Okay. We'll take the car and go back to the party. I'll drive Nana to St. Mary's, and you stay with your mother and help Ermaline and Sherman send the guests home and clean up. . . . St. Mary's . . . where is St. Mary's?"

Dad is running me through the carnival. Just outside the entrance I see our Ford. It's parked all crooked, and one door is even open.

"Get in," says Dad.

I climb in beside him.

"Now tell me how Adam wound up at the carnival tonight."

I stare down at my hands and mumble the truth.

"What?" says Dad.

"I asked him to come with me so he wouldn't have to spend the evening alone in his room," I say loudly. "It seemed mean."

"Did you ask Nana and Papa's permission to do that?" Dad glances at me, and I shake my head.

"Why?"

"Because I thought they'd say no."

Dad looks straight ahead as he sends our car careening out of the parking lot and heads it toward Nana and Papa's house. He doesn't say anything. He doesn't have to. I know what he is thinking. And I know I am in big trouble.

Seventeen

There are days when I wish I didn't live in a stupid board-inghouse, when I wish I could wake up like a normal person without listening to a thousand cuckoo clocks, without running into Mr. Penny in the hallway before he has shaved, without having to make Miss Hagerty's breakfast. Some days I would like to smash Mr. Penny's clocks and Miss Hagerty's dusty knickknacks. And I would like to sit down at breakfast with my mother and my father and no one else and also not have to look at Angel Valentine who is more beautiful than I'll ever be.

I feel like this almost every day during the week after Adam falls apart on the Ferris wheel.

On Sunday evening, not twenty-four hours after the police-men take him away, Adam comes home from the hospital. I think the doctors might have wanted him to stay longer, but Papa has a chat with them, makes an enormous donation to the hospital, and the next thing we know, he's driving Adam home.

Everyone is furious at me.

Mom and Dad have several talks with me on Sunday. The night before, when Mom and I were helping Ermaline and Sherman with the ruined party, Mom would not talk to me at all. She makes up for that the next day.

"Do you have any idea what you did last night, Hattie?" she asks.

It is late morning. We are in the parlor. Mom and Dad are on the couch, sitting squished together at one end like they need each other for protection. I am cross-legged in an armchair.

"I know I shouldn't have told Adam to sneak out of the house," I say, "but what does that have to do with anything? He's been to the carnival before. He just never wanted to go on any rides."

"Hattie," says Dad, "you are treading on thin ice."

I open my mouth, then close it.

"Adam is Nana and Papa's child," says Mom.

"He's not a child," I tell her.

"Hattie," says Dad.

"In some ways he is a child," says Mom. "But in any case, you do not make decisions about him. That is up to Nana and Papa. And I think you know that, Hattie, or you would have asked permission to take Adam to the carnival. Why didn't you ask permission?"

"Because Nana and Papa would have said no." I say this with a huge sigh.

"And why do you think they would have said no?"

I want to say, "Because they're mean," but I know better. I shake my head. "I don't know."

"Because that's too much for Adam — going out at night to a carnival . . . so much stimulation and excitement. . . ." Mom's voice trails off, like maybe she is remembering something.

"It would have been all right if the Ferris wheel hadn't gotten stuck," I say.

Mom just shakes her head at me.

"Hattie," says Dad, "even if the Ferris wheel hadn't gotten stuck, what do you think would have happened if Nana and Papa had gone upstairs during the party and discovered that Adam was missing?"

"I don't know."

"You really were not thinking," says Dad.

"Well, none of you were thinking about Adam. You never are."

"Believe me, I am always thinking about Adam," says Mom tightly.

*   *   *

"What were you thinking?" Nana asks me.

It is Sunday night. Adam is at home. I am already in trouble with Mom and Dad, and not allowed to leave the house until Saturday. Now Nana has come over, and it is her turn to have a talk with me.

What was I thinking? How can I tell Nana what I was thinking?

"I just thought Adam would want to have fun last night," I say. I am squirming in my seat.

"You thought you knew better? Better than Papa? Better than I?"

I shrug. "Maybe," I say, and I see Nana's face harden. "Adam wants to have fun just like anyone else," I tell her. "But you keep him hidden away in his room. You and Papa want to live your lives and pretend that Adam doesn't have any problems —"

"Hattie!" exclaims Nana, and she slams the palm of her hand onto a table, knocking a china dish to the floor.

I look at her, sitting primly in our parlor, her legs crossed at her ankles. She is wearing a pale blue summer suit, complete with gloves and the hat with the bird on it.

"Hattie," she says again, and she leans down to retrieve the dish. When she has set it carefully on the table she continues. "I don't know how last night's plan came up, but I

143

have a good idea. And that is why you are forbidden to go to the carnival again."

"What?"

"You never did things like this before you met that circus child —"

"Leila? This isn't Leila's fault!"

"Excuse me, Harriet, I am speaking."

"Sorry."

"And what I say goes. No more carnival."

"But Leila doesn't have a phone. I have to see her so at least I can tell her —"

Nana looks at me so sharply that I stop speaking. "That is my final word," she says. She stands up. "Last night could have been a lot worse, Hattie. You don't know."

I glare at Nana. After a moment I say, "Can I see him?" Nana looks confused so I say, "*Adam.* Can I see Adam? I want to find out how he's doing."

"He's all right. He needs time to calm down. I don't want the two of you to see each other just now."

"Fine," I say, and fling myself out of the armchair, run to my room, and slam the door.

There's no use asking Mom and Dad to talk to Nana about her punishment. They won't stand up to her. They never do. This is why I decide I am not going to speak to Nana or Papa or my parents.

What Leila and I did was wrong. But now I have been put in the middle of something else entirely. Something about Adam and the adults and things that happened before I was born, maybe even before Adam and Uncle Hayden and Mom were born.

I decide that I hate my family.

It is Wednesday when the Strowskys arrive. I am sitting on our front porch steps, chewing on a strand of hair, not help-ing Cookie in the kitchen, wondering how Adam is feeling over in that huge house with Nana and Papa, and wishing Mom and Dad and Nana and Papa were all dead and that I could live with Angel Valentine, whose looks I decide I could put up with. Also, I am composing a letter to Leila in my head and trying to figure out what the mailing address for the carnival would be.

I am sitting on the top step chewing and staring when a Ford station wagon that is even older and more battered than ours pulls up at the end of our walk. A woman is driving. Crowded next to her in the front seat are a boy and a girl. The entire rest of the car is jammed with suitcases and cartons.

The woman gets out of the car. She's holding a piece of paper. She looks at the paper, looks up at our house, looks back at the paper. Then she closes the car door, leans in the window, and says something to the kids.

I spit out my hair and stand up as the woman starts to

walk toward our house. She holds up her hand to shade her eyes from the sun.

"Hello," she calls to me. "Is this the Owen boardinghouse?"

"Yes," I say.

"Do you live here?"

"Yes."

"Do you know if there are any rooms to let?"

"Well," I say, "not really." All the rooms are full. Only our own guest room is empty and that's pretty small.

"Oh." The woman drops her hand and turns around.

I look back at the car and see the boy and girl watching us through an open window.

"Wait," I say. "You should talk to my parents, though."

Which means that *I* will have to talk to them, and I have not said one word to them in almost three whole days.

I am madder at my mother than I am at my father, so I run upstairs to Dad's studio, pound on the door, and yell, "There's someone downstairs to see you. She needs a room."

By the time I run back to the porch, the woman is sitting on a chair, and the boy and girl are sitting together on the swing. The girl looks like she's about my age; the boy is a little younger. They have the reddest hair and the saddest faces I have ever seen. The three of them are absolutely silent, just waiting.

"My dad will be out in a minute," I say.

And in about three minutes Dad walks through the door, followed by Mom. Dad is dusting off his hands on his pants, and Mom is wiping her hands on her apron.

"I'm Jonathan Owen," says Dad, "and this is my wife, Dorothy. Can we help you?"

The woman has stood up. She holds her hand out to Dad and says, "My name is Barbara Strowsky. This is my daughter, Catherine, and my son, Sam." Mrs. Strowsky points to the two kids, who glance up but still don't smile. "We . . . we need a place to stay for a while. We're just . . ." Her eyes have filled with tears.

"Why don't you come inside?" says Mom, reaching for her hand. "Hattie, you stay out here with Catherine and Sam. See if they'd like some lemonade."

By that evening the Strowskys have moved in. They are staying in our guest room, all crowded together, Mrs. Strowsky and Catherine in the double bed, Sam on the roll-away cot that we keep in our attic.

And I am talking to Mom and Dad again. I had to talk to them if I wanted to hear the Strowskys' story.

Which is a sad one. They lived down in Maryland until a couple of days ago. But Mr. Strowsky died suddenly this summer, and Mrs. Strowsky decided she couldn't stay on in their old house, their old town. So she loaded up the car and drove north looking for a place where she and Catherine and Sam could start over.

"They don't know a soul here," Mom tells me. "And they hardly have two cents. Mrs. Strowsky is going to look for a job."

"How come they came to Millerton?" I ask. "Are they going to stay here?"

Dad shrugs. "They're not sure yet. I think they want to see how they like it. We told them they could live rent-free in the guest room for a month until they decide what they want to do."

"Mrs. Strowsky is going to start job-hunting tomorrow," Mom adds.

I think that means Catherine and Sam will be out and about in our house all day while their mother is gone, but I am wrong. I only see them at meals. They are the quietest kids I have ever met.

For the rest of that week they keep to themselves, and I keep to myself. I brood about Adam. For the first time since he arrived in Millerton I wonder what he does at his house all day long. I try to remember when *I Love Lucy* is on TV. I am sure Adam watches it. But what else does he do? And how does he behave when he's at home? What do he and Nana and Papa talk about? Do they talk?

I realize I hardly know my uncle at all.

At the same time, I suddenly see that Adam and I are so alike, we could be brother and sister.

Eighteen

On Saturday, my parents' punishment ends, so I'm allowed to leave our house. But Nana's punishment doesn't have an end, as far as I can tell, so I can't go to the carnival.

That morning the weatherman says it's going to be a hot one, the hottest day of the summer so far. By noon our backyard thermometer reads 102. It's in the sun, though, so I figure that on our porch it is probably only 99 or 100 degrees. I take a Popsicle from our freezer and sit on the porch swing, trying to decide what to do. Adam's box is in my pocket, rattling with change. I could walk downtown, but the heat is hanging heavy all around, and somehow I don't feel like talking to the Finches or Mr. Shucard or Mrs. Moore.

Anyway, what I really want to do is see Adam, but I don't know whether I'm allowed. And the only person who could tell me whether I'm allowed is Nana, and I am not about to call her.

Our house is awfully quiet. Mom and Dad are at the grocery store, Miss Hagerty is napping in her room, Mr. Penny is out somewhere, and I don't know where Angel Valentine is. I am just wondering what the Strowskys are doing, when the screen door swings silently open and Catherine steps onto the porch.

"Hi," I say. I lick dripping Popsicle juice from my hand.

"Hi," she replies. For a moment she hesitates, and I think she might go back inside. Instead, she sits down, very carefully, on the edge of a chair.

Here is one of those times when I have absolutely no idea what to say, but I realize that Catherine doesn't either. I think that maybe she is even shyer than I am.

"I've hardly seen you since Wednesday," I say at last.

"I've been taking care of Sam when Mom's out."

"But you're allowed to come out of your room, you know. There's a television in the parlor. And if you go outside, there's a swing set in the backyard. For Sam, I mean."

"Really?" Catherine gives me a small smile.

"Sure."

"Well . . . thanks."

"It's okay. I was wondering . . . maybe you'll still be here when school starts. . . . What grade will you be in?"

"Seventh," says Catherine.

"Me too! So we might be in the same class."

I am studying Catherine's red curls, which are actually bright, bright orange, when over her shoulder I see a jaunty figure come whistling up our front walk.

"Adam!" I exclaim.

"A great good afternoon to you, Hattie Owen!" he says.

Adam is in a fine mood, I can tell. And I'm surprised. I suppose because the last time I saw him he was kicking and hitting and being dragged away by policemen. He smiles and waves, and I see that he is carrying a bouquet of flowers. At the bottoms of the stems are roots and dirt, and I think he has pulled them directly out of Nana's garden.

Adam bounces up the porch steps and stands in front of me. He is wearing a suit and a necktie, and he looks quite handsome, but he must be absolutely boiling, because he is wearing his woolen winter suit.

He opens his mouth, but before he can say anything, Catherine jumps to her feet, says, "I'd better go," and disappears through the porch door.

Adam looks after her for a moment, then turns to me and grins. "Today is a tip-top, first-rate, one-of-a-kind, shining day, Hattie, and so I have come to call on Miss Angel Valentine. Is she at home?"

Oh, I think, the flowers are for Angel.

I give Adam a big smile, try to ignore the soil that is dropping from the roots of the flowers and onto his shined penny loafers.

"Gosh, Adam," I say. "I'm not sure. Do you want to wait here while I go knock on her door?"

"Thank you very much, mademoiselle, but I will come with you," Adam replies.

I pause with my hand on the door. I'm not sure Angel is at home, and if she is, she might still be asleep. I have seen her sleep awfully late on weekend mornings. I'm about to say this to Adam when he gives me a small shove to the side, pulls open the screen door, and marches into our hallway. "Come on, Hattie, but tread carefully, tread softly, you don't want to waken Mrs. Trumbull, Little Ricky is noisy enough." He puffs up the stairs, trailing dirt behind him.

I run after Adam, not quiet at all. When we reach Angel's door, I put out my hand to knock on it. I have not even touched the door, though, when Adam thrusts his hand under my arm, turns the knob, and throws the door open.

"Adam!" I cry, and at the same time I hear a small shriek from inside the room and see Angel tumble from her bed to the floor.

She was still asleep after all, I think, but then I realize that Angel is dressed, or at least partly dressed, and that is when I see Henry lying on the bed, wearing pants but no shirt.

"Oh, my God," I say under my breath.

Angel says nothing. She has scrambled to her feet and is trying to button her blouse.

I look at Adam. He is looking at Angel, his mouth open like a character in a cartoon, and I know exactly what he is thinking. We are so alike, Adam and I, our brains are so alike, that Adam's thoughts are in my head now. Adam is thinking that at long last he has seen Angel's actual chest without any clothing to cover it. He is fascinated by her fingers as they fumble with the buttons of the blouse. He feels about 10 percent satisfied at having caught her doing something she shouldn't be doing in our house, 20 percent horrified by his own bad behavior, and 70 percent excited by what we have interrupted.

My mouth grows dry, and my heart starts to pound. I can't stop looking at Angel either, looking at this scene we have disturbed, this thing that boyfriends and girlfriends do in private.

Adam stares at Angel for so long that I begin to be afraid he might barge into the room. But he doesn't. Instead, I see the flowers fall from his hands, and he lets out an animal wail. Then he runs down the hall toward the stairs.

I am right after him.

"Hey, hey," I call.

Adam won't stop. He has almost reached the bottom of the stairs.

I hesitate for a moment, then turn back to Angel's room. I reach it as she is about to close the door, so I stick my foot in the crack.

"What —" Angel starts to say.

I look at her crooked blouse, her wild hair, glance through the crack, see Henry sitting half-naked on the bed, and no words will come. So I remove my foot, and pull her door shut with such force that the walls shake.

Then I go after Adam.

I look up and down the street in front of our house and I don't see him, but I am pretty certain he has headed home, so I run all the way to Nana and Papa's. As I round the corner to their street I see Adam charge through the front door.

I am panting and so sweaty, I feel slippery, but I don't stop running. I ring Nana and Papa's bell, then turn the knob before anyone answers. Nana is standing in the hallway, her hands on the banister, looking up the stairs to the second floor.

She turns around when I close the door behind me.

"Hattie, what's going on?" she says, and I think she looks afraid.

I try to catch my breath. "Adam came over to see Angel Valentine, so we went upstairs, and he opened the door to her room without knocking, and Angel was in there with her boyfriend, and he's really upset because he was going to give her flowers —"

"Why on earth did you take Adam upstairs, Hattie?"

"Well —"

"You know better."

I stare at Nana. "You keep saying that," I say finally. "Everyone keeps saying that. But why don't *you* know better about Adam? He's your son."

"Harriet!"

What I don't say is the awful thing that has just worked its way into my head. That I actually *should* know better. That Adam and I are so similar that half the time now I know what he's thinking. I am like Adam and I do not want to be like Adam.

Nana has set her mouth in a firm line. She brushes at a lock of gray hair, and I see that her hand is shaking. "Hattie, you don't understand him," she says quietly.

But I do.

I open Nana's front door.

"Where are you going?" she asks.

"To the carnival," I say. "You are not my mother. Or my father. And I don't have to listen to you."

I slam the door behind me and run across the lawn.

It is time to talk to Leila.

Nineteen

The first thing I notice when I arrive at Fred Carmel's is that the parking lot is nearly empty. Well, I think, most everybody around here has already been to the carnival. Still, this *is* Saturday. . . . Then I see that a wooden sawhorse has been placed across the entrance. I stand at the sawhorse and peer ahead.

What a strange day this has been. My house was too quiet this morning, and now the carnival is way too quiet.

I shade my eyes with a sweaty hand. I don't see much, but after a moment I hear some banging, like the sound of workmen. And then I see a couple of trucks driving around the carnival grounds. The only time I ever saw a vehicle inside the carnival was when the ambulance came for Adam last weekend.

The sawhorse has been put up as a barrier to keep people out of the carnival, but I climb over it anyway. I don't think anyone will mind if I come in to look for Leila. I haven't walked very far when I realize that the reason the carnival is so quiet is because it is closing down. The rides are still. The game booths are nearly empty, the last of the prizes that hung on the walls being packed away. And the only people walking around are Leila's relatives and the other workers. They are so busy taking things down and packing things up that they don't notice me.

With a tight feeling in my chest I make my way to the Cahns' trailer. I walk and walk, but I can't find it, and now I am sure I am standing exactly where the trailer should be parked. Maybe the trailers have been moved to another part of the carnival, I think. I am wondering where that might be when I hear someone call my name.

"Hattie!"

I see Leila's uncle Jace striding toward me, a hammer in his hand.

"Hey!" I exclaim. "Hi. I was just looking for Leila. I hope it's okay that I came in."

"It's all right," says Jace, "but Leila isn't here anymore."

My chest tightens a little further. "What do you mean?"

"They've gone ahead. To Maryland."

"Gone ahead?"

"The carnival's going to be outside of Bethesda for the next few weeks. We're closing here and we'll be on our way tomorrow. But Leila and Lamar and their folks left yesterday. They're going to visit Leila's aunt for a day or two before we get set up again."

I cannot think of a single word to say.

"Hattie?" says Jace.

I shake my head. I am not about to cry in front of him. I start to run.

"Hattie!" I hear Jace call.

I run and run and run. I run through the carnival, through the parking lot, and all the way to Marquand Park, where, if I am lucky, nobody will be sitting on the bench by the duck pond and I will have it to myself for a while.

The park is not deserted like the carnival is; still, not many people are around. Too hot, I think. I slide onto the empty bench and watch the ducks trail around in the murky water.

Two words slip into my head.

Damn Nana.

I have never thought such words before. But there they are.

Leila is gone, and I didn't get to say good-bye to her, didn't get to explain why I couldn't see her all week. And it is Nana's fault. Does Leila think I am mad at her? Does she think I blame her for what happened?

I feel tears prick at my eyes but I don't let them fall until I am certain that no one is nearby, and that even the ducks have turned their backs.

I sit there and cry and cry as silently as possible, finally wiping my eyes and nose with the back of my hand like I am three years old.

The only thing that makes me feel a little better is realizing that Leila's uncle and the others are still here in Millerton, will certainly be here until tomorrow at least. So I can write a letter to Leila, tell her everything, tell her good-bye, tell her I'll miss her, tell her she was one of the few friends I ever made. And I can take the letter to Jace in the morning and he can give it to Leila in Maryland.

I sit there for a long time, writing the letter in my head. *Dear Leila, My grandmother wouldn't let me see you last week because you are a circus child. And I couldn't call you because you don't have a phone. And I never even invited you over, so you don't know where I live.*

What kind of friends were Leila and I anyway? What kind of friend was I?

I sigh, look around for something to toss to the ducks, and see a piece of bread they have overlooked. I throw it into the pond, but don't stay to watch the ducks discover it. I walk home, taking the longest possible route, since I am absolutely positive Nana has called my parents by now to tell them what I have done, to say, "What was Hattie thinking?"

My long, long route eventually takes me down an avenue that intersects with Nana and Papa's street. When I reach their corner I tell myself to stare straight ahead, not even to glance at their house. But a police cruiser turns the corner and I just have to see where it is going. I stand at the curb and watch. And it pulls into Nana and Papa's driveway. Before its engine has even been turned off, a policeman jumps out of the passenger side, slams the door shut, and hurries along the front walk. Papa meets him at the door.

I do not know whether I am welcome at Nana and Papa's now, but I have to find out what is going on. I reach their front door just as the officer who had been driving the cruiser leaps up the porch steps in one bound.

"Papa?" I say.

Papa is standing in the open doorway talking to the officers. Nana is hovering behind him in the front hall.

"Hattie!" exclaims Nana. "Thank God."

"What? What?" I say.

"Have you seen Adam?" Papa asks me.

"Adam? I thought he came home."

"He did," says Nana. "But he left not long after that, and he was so upset. . . . I called your parents. They haven't seen him all day. I've called everywhere. I was hoping he was with you."

"No. I haven't seen him either. I mean, not since he ran back here."

"Where have you been all afternoon?" Papa asks. He grips my shoulder so hard, it hurts, and I back away from him.

"I — I went to the carnival first, but it's closed." I shoot an angry look at Nana. "And then I went to Marquand Park, and then I walked around town."

"And you didn't see Adam anywhere?" says one of the officers.

"No."

The policemen and Nana and Papa look at one another.

"I think we'd better come inside, Mr. Mercer," says one of the officers. He pulls a notepad out of his pocket.

"Hattie, you go on home," says Nana. "Go straight home."

"Okay," I say.

Adam is a grown-up, and technically he has not been gone long enough to be considered a missing person. On the other hand, Adam is Adam, and he is the son of Hayden and Harriet Mercer, so the search for him begins immediately. The police go off in their cruiser. Mom and Dad drive around in our Ford.

I am told to stay at home.

"Why couldn't I go with them?" I ask Miss Hagerty as we have a cup of tea in her room. Miss Hagerty has made the tea this time, and she keeps telling me how soothing and relaxing tea can be in times of stress.

It is late evening. Cookie stayed past her quitting time in order to serve dinner to Mr. Penny and Miss Hagerty and the Strowskys and me.

I notice that Angel Valentine is nowhere to be seen.

"I'm sure your parents want you at home in case Adam turns up here," Miss Hagerty replies.

I'm not so sure. I think Nana has decided that I can't be trusted with Adam after all. I think she wants me out of the way.

"Miss Hagerty, what is wrong with Adam?"

Miss Hagerty puts down her teacup and looks at me for a long time. "You know, I'm not sure, Dearie. I don't think anyone has ever told me. He's just . . . funny." Miss Hagerty taps the side of her head. "I believe you would say he is mentally ill."

I sigh. Funny. Mentally ill. These words are not helpful. I decide not to ask Miss Hagerty if mental illness can run in a family.

When we have finished our tea, it is time for Miss Hagerty to begin her beauty regime. I take our cups downstairs to the kitchen. Later I sit on the front porch and look at the moon. I'm pretty sure Angel Valentine is not home. When she does come back, I hope Mom and Dad give her a good talking-to.

I am still looking at the moon when the front door opens and someone settles beside me on the porch swing.

Catherine.

"I'm sorry about your uncle," she says.

I glance at her. "Thanks." I don't know how much she knows about Adam. "He has some problems."

"I bet they'll find him soon."

"Probably."

Catherine looks at the moon with me.

"I'm sorry about your father," I say at last.

"He had a heart attack. He went to work like usual one day, and then his boss found him slumped over his desk. He was dead."

I nod. Catherine and I have both found out how quickly our world can swing between what is comfortable and familiar and what is unexpected and horrifying.

At nine-thirty Mrs. Strowsky calls Catherine inside. I continue to sit on the swing. I look at my watch about every five minutes. Almost ten-fifteen and Mom and Dad still have not come home. Finally I go upstairs to bed. I have just fallen asleep when I hear my door open, and light from the hallway falls across my face.

"Hattie?" says Mom.

I sit up, immediately wide awake. "Did you find him?"

Dad appears behind her in the doorway. They step into

my room, and before they have even sat on my bed I know that they have news for me and it is very bad.

I put my hands over my ears. "Don't tell me," I say. "I don't want to hear it."

Very gently, Mom pulls my hands down. Then she gathers me against her. I can feel Dad stroking my hair.

"The police found Adam," says Mom.

"He's dead, isn't he?"

Mom doesn't answer, and I feel her tears on my cheek.

"He is, Hattie," says Dad.

"What happened?"

"He hung himself. In the shed behind Nana and Papa's."

I am sad. But I am not very surprised.

Twenty

My uncle Hayden is sitting in our parlor with his pipe clenched between his teeth. He smells like the back of Cline's, where they sell the tobacco and cigarettes.

It was shortly after dinner the next night when Mom answered a knock on our front door. "Oh, my God," I heard her say. "Hayden."

I poked my head out of the dining room to see a tall man standing in shadow beyond our screen door, and I watched my mother cross the front hall. She started off in slow motion but was running by the time she reached the door. She put her arms around her brother, and they hugged for a long time.

We did not expect Uncle Hayden to arrive so soon. Mom had called him the night before, shortly after eleven, and he had said he would take the next flight east. Even so, Mom hadn't expected him until Monday.

But here he is on Sunday, at the end of the longest day of my life.

Time has been passing the way it did when I was six and got the measles and had to stay in bed forever. Each day felt like three days, six days, weeks. The night Adam's body is found, we are up until nearly two o'clock. Half the house is up with us. Miss Hagerty hears us talking and emerges from her room, with what she calls Oil of Delay smeared on her face, and her hair tied up in a threadbare kerchief. We walk downstairs together, and Miss Hagerty sits with Mom on the sofa in the parlor. Later Mrs. Strowsky wakes up and joins us. Nobody says much. Mom is nearly silent, not even crying, but looking bewildered and bruised.

And then Angel Valentine comes home. I think maybe she had hoped to be able to slip inside without being noticed, but I catch sight of her tiptoeing up the stairs, carrying her shoes in one hand. She runs into Mr. Penny, who has heard the news too and is on his way downstairs. He meets Angel halfway and tells her what has happened.

I can't hear their conversation. All I know is that Angel goes on up to her room, and we don't see her again until the next day.

"I hope you tell her exactly what she has done," I say to Dad. "I hope you tell her she killed Adam."

Dad places his hand on my shoulder and says gently, "You know that isn't true, Hattie."

I do know that. But still.

Nobody sleeps that night. The next morning I drag myself out of bed at five-thirty, because there is just no point in lying around and staring at the ceiling anymore. It is Sunday, and people start dropping by our house as soon as breakfast is over. Although it is Cookie's day off, she shows up anyway, and that is a good thing, because everyone brings food. Our kitchen fills up with casseroles and cakes and pastries and even urns of coffee.

Cookie takes charge. She sorts out the food, wrapping some of it and putting it in our refrigerator or freezer. She puts the rest of it on plates and keeps handing the plates to Mrs. Strowsky and Catherine to pass to the people who have paused in our parlor to talk to Dad, then washes the empty plates when they bring them back.

Mom is upstairs in her bedroom. She stays there until almost noon. When I peek inside to see if she's all right I find her standing in front of her mirror, fixing herself up like she does for the Girls' Lunches. I can even smell perfume.

"What are you doing?" I ask.

"I ought to go over to Nana and Papa's," she says. "They'll have a houseful too."

Mom is staring intently at the mirror. I start to tell her that she looks fine, and then I realize that she is looking not at herself but at the photos she has stuck all around the edges of the mirror. Photos of me when I was a baby, my tiny school pictures, pictures of her and Dad, a picture of Dad when he was a baby, Uncle Hayden's college graduation picture, the yellowed photo of Nana and Papa that appeared in the newspaper when they announced their engagement.

"Mom," I say, "you don't have any pictures of Adam there."

"Huh," says Mom. "I guess not."

"Why don't you?"

A look of pain crosses her face but she only shrugs.

I think of a question I have been wanting to ask. "Did you ever visit Adam when he was at school?" I don't remember Mom taking any trips, but maybe she visited him when I was very little.

Mom sighs. "No. Nana and Papa visited him from time to time. On their trip to Chicago, their trip to Milwaukee, a few other times. But Nana asked me not to visit. She said it would upset Adam."

I frown. "Didn't you love him?" I ask.

Mom turns around sharply, hand raised. "Hattie," she says, "don't you ever ask me that question again."

I stumble backward, and Mom catches my arm. "I'm sorry, I'm sorry," she says. "Hattie, don't pay any attention to me." And then she adds, "Yes, I loved him. But he was very hard to love. . . . Do you want to come to Nana and Papa's with me?"

"Not really," I say, and leave the room.

The afternoon finally arrives and passes in the same endless fashion as the morning. More and more I find Adam creeping into my thoughts.

I accept a tuna casserole from a neighbor, say, "Thank you," and in my head hear Adam say, "Oh, ho, ho, ho! Tuna casserole, Hattie, a divine dish, fit for a king, fit for a king, Hattie Owen."

From the yard Sam Strowsky shouts something to Catherine, and for some reason I am back in Nana's dining room and Adam is stomping on the hidden buzzer.

I hold the front door open for another guest, glimpse the cloudless sky beyond the porch, and remember Adam whispering, "Because Mother says it's a circus trick."

I close the screen door, feel tears gathering.

"Ricky won't let Lucy have a new hat, Hattie Owen. Lucy must save money and make her own dress, Hattie. Oh, Ethel's birthday did not go well, not well at all. Lucy wrote a novel, Hattie Owen, Lucy wrote a play, Lucy wrote an operetta and Ricky sang, 'I am the good Prince Lancelot, I love to sing and dance a lot.'"

His voice is so loud in my head that I want to cover my ears like I did last night, cover them to keep out the sound of Adam. My new uncle, my family.

"You big baby," I say aloud. "You didn't have to leave that way, you know." He shouldn't have left at all. There was no reason for it.

Well, maybe there were some reasons, but they weren't good enough.

Five o'clock in the afternoon, Mom has left and come back, Cookie is still here, and I need a rest. I lie down on my bed. And that is when I remember the letter to Leila. I never wrote it, and clean forgot about going to Fred Carmel's this morning. The carnival is gone now, I am sure, even though its departure will have been without any fanfare, no parade like when it arrived; just pull up the stakes and disappear.

And so that is that. I have absolutely no idea how to get in touch with Leila.

Three hours later dinner is over and Uncle Hayden makes his surprise arrival. He hugs Mom, hugs Dad, hugs me, tells me he hardly recognizes me. Then he says to Mom, "How's Mother?"

Mom shrugs. "How you'd expect. Dry-eyed."

"Pinched?" says Hayden. "All kind of pinched and held in?"

I want to laugh, and I can't tell whether my mother does

too, but suddenly her hand flies to her mouth, and she says, "Oh, no, Hayden, I just realized. You can't stay here. You'll have to stay with Mother and Father." She tells him about the Strowskys and our extra-full house.

Uncle Hayden groans. That's when he sits down in the armchair in the parlor and clenches his pipe between his teeth. After a moment he takes the pipe out, stares across the room at nothing, and his eyes fill with tears. I don't know much about Uncle Hayden. Only that he never married and he works for one of the big movie companies. And he hasn't been to Millerton since before I was born.

Mom perches on the edge of Uncle Hayden's chair and rubs his shoulders. He looks up at her. "Tell me again what happened," he says.

"The school closed," Mom begins.

Adam's own brother didn't know he was home.

Do the people in my family *never* talk to each other?

But Uncle Hayden is back. He has come back. He is here for Mom, and for Nana and Papa too, I suppose. And of course for Adam.

Adam's funeral is to be held on Tuesday. His obituary appears in the Millerton paper on Monday. It says hardly anything about who Adam was, just the younger son of Hayden and Harriet Mercer, twenty-one years old. It doesn't even say the name of the school where he lived for so many years. No-body who reads the paper will know about Shirley Temples, or Lucy eating snails, or flowers plucked up by their roots and offered hopefully to a pretty girl. And nobody will know the Adam on the Ferris wheel, or that he was called a freak, or about his temper tantrums.

I want people to know.

And so I call my grandmother on the phone and say, "Nana, at the funeral tomorrow I want to say something."

"What? Say something to whom?"

"I want to speak." I must speak.

"But, Hattie —"

"Adam was my uncle, and I want to say something about him."

"All right," says Nana.

That night, Mom comes into my room and starts sliding the hangers back and forth in my closet.

"What are you looking for?" I ask her.

"Something black. Where's that dress you wore last Christmas?"

"It's too hot. It's velvet. And it doesn't fit."

I have decided what I am going to wear to the funeral. It's the yellow dress I wore to my family birthday party. Adam told me he liked it. He told me he liked it, and five minutes later he ate the rose off the cake and was sent outside.

Mom doesn't argue with me. She stands before my closet looking blank and muttering that she can't believe we are deciding what to wear to Adam's funeral and that people are not supposed to die before their parents do. I put my arm across her shoulders and she gives me a tiny smile, cups my chin in her hand for a moment, then hurries out of the room.

I lay the yellow dress on my armchair. I am looking around for my white flats when I see Angel Valentine hurry along the hall to her room.

I have not spoken to Angel since Saturday. She has not eaten a single meal with us. And she flits in and out of our house like a moth, silently. She did pause on Sunday, though, to tell Mom and Dad how very sorry she was for their loss, and to say something else, which I did not hear.

I do not believe she will be at the funeral.

Twenty-One

Tuesday, August 2, 1960, the day Adam Mercer is buried, is glorious. "A funeral day," says Cookie. "Haven't you noticed? Funeral days either pour down rain or pour forth sunshine. Nothing in between." I don't know about that. But this morning is clear and warm and sweet, with a whisper of wind that shakes the leaves in the elm tree outside my window. It is a day that might have made Adam cry, "Happiness! Happiness!"

At ten-thirty I go to my room and quietly close the door behind me. I look for a long time at the yellow dress and my shoes, laid out for the day. After a while I slip the dress on, then the shoes. Nana will want me to wear gloves, but I don't plan to.

Mom and Dad and I set off for the Episcopalian church just after eleven o'clock. Miss Hagerty and Mr. Penny and

Cookie and even Mrs. Strowsky are going to go to Adam's funeral, but they are going to leave a little later, so that my parents and I can walk there on our own.

When we arrive at the church we see that the parking lot is already nearly full.

"Wow," I say softly.

When Hayden and Harriet Mercer give a funeral, everybody comes.

That is what I think until I see Nancy and Janet in the crowd. They are not here because of my grandparents. They are here purely out of curiosity. They want to see the freak's family. They want to see what kind of funeral the freak will have. As if we are an attraction at Fred Carmel's sideshow. I wonder if any of Nana and Papa's friends feel the same way.

Dad sees me eyeing Nancy and Janet, sees them eyeing me back, sees their contained giggles. He takes me by the elbow. "Come on, Hattie."

We make our way through the crowd and into the hushed church. Dad loops his arms through Mom's and mine and we walk to the front, slide into the very first pew next to Nana and Papa and Uncle Hayden. We make a row, the six of us.

The church is hot, the church is full of shushings and loud quiet, the church is rustling and whispering and waiting, and after a while I don't hear anything but Adam. "Oh, ho, ho, ho, Hattie Owen."

I jump a little when the organ begins to play, jump again when, after the last note has wheezed out, the priest speaks. He talks and talks about Adam, and truthfully, he could be saying his words about practically any person in the room. Well, of course, I think. The priest has only been at this church for seven years. He probably never even met Adam.

When he has finished speaking he suggests that we bow our heads in prayer, and I whisper to Mom, "Let me move down to the end."

Nana frowns at me. I ignore her.

I do not know whether Nana has told the priest that I want to say something about Adam. I am prepared to stand up on the pew and just start talking, if necessary. But when the prayer is over, the priest looks at me and nods. Then he leaves the microphone at the front of the church and sits off to the side.

My legs wobble, and my breath comes in shallow gasps as I slip out of the pew and climb the steps to the pulpit. I have not prepared what I am going to say, and now I think maybe that was a mistake.

The microphone is much too high for me, so I lower it and it squeals and I hear giggles. I have told myself to find Miss Hagerty in the crowd and talk directly to her, but the giggles help me locate Nancy and Janet, and I decide that I will talk to them instead.

"My name is Harriet Owen," I begin. "I am Adam Mercer's niece."

I glance at Nana, and she looks as though she is holding her breath. I look away, back to Nancy and Janet. "I am Adam Mercer's niece," I say again. "And I want you to know that Adam was not a freak."

I hear a sound, as if every person in the church has just sucked in his breath. I look only at Nancy and Janet, though, and I see them drop their eyes.

"But he was called a freak," I say. "He was called lots of names. And that was one of the things that made it hard to be Adam."

I talk about other things that upset Adam — confusion and too much noise and fears I don't understand. I talk about Lucy Ricardo and dancing and receiving an invitation to my own birthday party. I think about mentioning Adam's circus trick, but change my mind.

"Adam," I say, "had good times and he had bad times." I pause here and glance at Nana, see that she is crying silently, the way I cried at the duck pond in the park. I was going to say something more about the bad times — how Adam's bad times were different from most people's, and that I'll never really understand them. But now that I see Nana's tears, see her start to reach for Papa's hand, then pull back and fold her hands in her lap again — now that I see Nana, I change my mind.

"I think we should remember that Adam was one of those people who lift the corners of our universe," I say. I clear my throat. "Thank you."

As I slide into our pew I realize I feel older. I think of Janet and Nancy and find that now I can brush them away. And I understand that Adam and I are not as alike as I had thought. I remember the tortured look on Adam's face the night of the Ferris wheel and the look of happiness, happiness, and realize that Adam's decision to take his life was not made easily. It took a certain kind of courage. Just not the kind of courage I choose.

I settle between Mom and Dad, and they take my hands and smile at me. No tears. I squeeze their hands.

There is a sort of party at Nana and Papa's after the funeral. About a hundred people show up. They've come straight from the church and are still wearing their dark clothes. I am glowing in my yellow dress.

I walk around the house for a while, eating tiny hors d'oeuvres and drinking lemonade. If this were my house I'd retreat to the kitchen to help Cookie. But I don't know Ermaline well enough to do that. Eventually I need to use the bathroom, but the powder room on the first floor is occupied. As I climb the stairs to the second floor, I realize I never saw Adam's room.

I have to see it.

I trail along the hallway. I pass a guest room, a bathroom, another guest room, and then I come to a room with a partly closed door. I push the door open a few inches. The first thing I notice is that the walls and even the ceiling are almost entirely covered with pages that have been torn from magazines. Most of them are pictures of the moon and sun and stars, surely from *National Geographic*. Some of them are pictures of Lucille Ball and Desi Arnaz. I take a step into the room and let out a gasp.

Nana is sitting on the bed, legs crossed primly, fingering the contents of a wooden box that she has set on her knees. She looks up, as startled as I am.

"Hattie!" she says.

"Nana! I'm — I'm sorry." I start to back into the hall. "I was on my way to the bathroom."

"That's all right." Nana pats the bed. "Come in, Hattie."

I'm intruding, I know, but Nana has issued an invitation. I perch beside her on Adam's bed, eye the box.

"What's that?" I ask.

"It's Adam's treasure box."

Inside are small items — a rock, a blue feather, an Indian head nickel, and photos. Mostly photos.

"Your mother sent him something every week," she says. "Every single week for all those years he was at school. Little presents, pictures he might like for his room, photos of you. And Adam kept everything she sent."

"Did she write him letters?" I ask.

Nana nods. "Adam kept those too."

I think of Mom's mirror, the border of photos, hear her say, "Don't you ever ask me that question again."

I reach for Nana's hand. She sets the box aside, and we sit in Adam's room for a long time.

The day before Uncle Hayden leaves, my family decides to visit Adam's grave. Charles the chauffeur drives us there. We glide silently along the lane through the cemetery until Papa tells Charles to stop. Even though there was no burial service, everyone except me has seen the grave already. It looks fresher than the other graves, all clean and tidy, the grass neatly clipped, the flowers only a little wilted.

I tell Adam I'm sorry I called him a big baby. "I'm not mad at you, you know," I add. "I don't like what you did, but I think I understand why you did it."

I find that I can't go any closer to Adam's headstone, so I sit down in the grass a few yards away. Mom and Dad are holding hands. Uncle Hayden puts his arm across Mom's shoulders. I see Papa reach for Nana. And I see Nana's quiet tears for Adam.

Twenty-Two

I replace the reel of film in its canister, lean back in the armchair, feel October around me. Two months ago, time was like an old tired dog creeping along until finally he can't walk any further and he drops to his haunches on the sidewalk and just sits.

How is it that suddenly it's autumn and we have moved ahead? When did time pick up again, push forward?

I remember that in those blurry days following Adam's death, Angel moves out. Moves out quickly. One day she packs up her suitcases and two cardboard cartons from the supermarket, scribbles down a mailing address and gives it to my parents, then waits on our front porch for Henry to come by in his convertible. It occurs to me then that the convertible is part of the reason Adam is dead. I didn't see the convertible on the day Adam showed up with his flowers for Angel. If I had, I wouldn't have let Adam go upstairs. But Henry wasn't supposed to be upstairs with Angel in the first place, since that would have been against our rules, which is probably why the car wasn't parked nearby.

It takes me a long time to shake the feeling that Angel and her sneaking around are what killed Adam.

I don't look at the piece of paper Angel gives Mom and Dad, but I know Angel moves somewhere nearby — maybe with Henry — because twice now I have seen her going to her job at the bank. I haven't spoken to her yet, but someday I will.

The week after Uncle Hayden returns to California is the beginning of a long, bad time for Nana and Papa. I had thought they would put Adam behind them and get on with their lives as though nothing had happened, would erase Adam as easily as he had been erased while he was at school. And so I expect Papa to go back to work on Monday.

But he doesn't. Nana calls Mom late that morning to say that Papa is all dressed in his office clothes and is sitting upstairs in Adam's room staring at the walls and ceiling. He has been there since they finished breakfast. Mom and Dad hurry over to Nana and Papa's, but there doesn't seem to be anything for them to do. Eventually, Papa closes the door to Adam's room and fixes himself a martini, which he drinks alone, in the back garden.

Papa does this every day that week until Nana loses her patience with him and says it's time to clean out Adam's room, in particular to try to unstick everything from the walls and ceiling. Probably they will need to have the room repainted when this has been done.

Papa doesn't answer her, but he goes back to his office the next Monday and stops drinking martinis in the garden unless it's after 5:00 P.M.

The day Papa returns to work, Nana rejoices, calls to tell us the good news, and asks me if I will come over to give her a hand with Adam's room. I wonder why Nana doesn't ask one of the maids to help her, but I decide she doesn't want anyone except family taking a close look at Adam's things. An hour later I am once again in Adam's room with Nana.

"I guess we should start with the walls," I say. "We'll need a ladder to get the pictures off of the ceiling." I reach for a photo of Lucy Ricardo. She is looking at Ricky, who is stepping through the door to their apartment, and you can tell by her face that she has just done something sneaky that she doesn't want Ricky to find out about. The picture makes me smile, and I know why Adam liked Lucy. She is completely imperfect.

I pull at a corner of the photo and it tears and Nana lets out a cry. "No! Don't touch that."

"But I thought —"

"Never mind. Go home, Hattie."

So I do. It is another month before Nana decides Adam's room can be touched, and after all that, she borrows Toby diAngeli from us and lets her clean it out, and then hires Nassau Interiors to redecorate the room, and by early October not a trace of Adam is left in the house. But if Adam's name is mentioned, Nana will burst into tears. And Papa is likely to reach for the bottle of vermouth.

In August, three days after Papa finally goes back to work, my parents announce that we are going to take a family trip. I am stunned.

"How can we do that?" I ask. We have never left our boarders.

"We are going to leave Cookie in charge. Everything will be fine," Mom says firmly.

And so we go to the beach town of Avalon, New Jersey, for three days. We rent a small cottage, one of a row of four small cottages a block from the beach, and we spend the days eating fried clams and baking in the sun. Each of us seems to need time alone. Dad leaves Mom and me early every morning to eat breakfast by himself at the counter at Hoy's. Mom finds the movie theater and goes to the same movie three days in a row. I am given money to rent a bicycle, and I ride all over town, just ride and ride.

But we play miniature golf together. And every night we

eat dinner in a restaurant together. And when dinner is over we walk to the beach in the dark and hold hands and look at the stars. On the first night I say, as we're sitting in the damp sand, "Now each of us has to say one thing we want to remember about Adam."

Mom bursts into tears. Then I start to cry, and eventually I realize Dad is crying too.

So we don't talk about Adam that night. But the next night, Mom says, "Adam was brave." And Dad says, "Adam could see right into your soul." And I say, "Adam was different." And my parents look at me but don't ask what I mean.

On the third night, our last night in Avalon, I say as we gaze at the stars, "Tonight we have to think of something we learned from Adam."

Mom says slowly, "Adam taught me that we should take time to enjoy life. And that it's okay to go against the grain. That's why we're here."

Here in this little place Nana wouldn't approve of, I think.

Dad just says, "Ditto."

And I say, "Adam taught me that we have to talk about things."

There is silence. Come on, come on, ask me what I meant when I said Adam was different. And if I have any other secret uncles, please tell me about them now.

But Mom just says, "Okay," and Dad says, "We'll try," and that is all I can hope for.

We are back in Millerton for the tail end of August. One afternoon Mrs. Strowsky comes home jubilant from job-hunting.

"I am going to be the head saleswoman in the children's department at Bamberger's!" she announces. "Imagine me, head anything."

She is all grinning and gay, and that night she takes Catherine and Sam to dinner at Renwick's and they get to eat hamburgers at the soda fountain counter. A week later they move to the tiny house Mrs. Strowsky is able to rent for them. When they leave, Catherine and I hug each other, and Catherine gives me her new phone number. "Come by to-morrow," she tells me. "I have my own room in the new house. You can help me fix it up."

So I do.

Just before Labor Day, Betsy comes home and I intro-duce her to Catherine, whom she has heard about from my letters, and before I know it we are a group of three. School starts, and Betsy and Catherine and I wind up in the same classroom. Nancy and Janet are in our class too, but I couldn't care less. They are not part of my universe.

On the first day of school we are not given any homework, so that night I write a letter to Leila. This is Catherine's idea.

"Just address it to Leila Cahn at Fred Carmel's Funtime Carnival in Bethesda. It might reach her," says Catherine.

"But the carnival wasn't going to be *in* Bethesda," I tell her. "It was going to be somewhere outside of it."

"How many Fred Carmel's Funtime Carnivals could there be anywhere *near* Bethesda?" asks Betsy, who has been listening to us.

She has a point.

So I write a letter to Leila that night and try to explain what happened, tell her about Adam, about Angel Valentine, about the funeral, and Nancy and Janet. I tell her she was a good friend.

I address the letter to Leila Cahn, c/o Fred Carmel's Funtime Carnival, Bethesda, MD. I put my return address in the upper-left corner of the envelope. The letter has not been returned to me, so maybe Leila has received it. Or maybe it will catch up with the carnival somehow.

I turn on the light, blink my eyes. Mom and Dad will be home soon. I slide the reel of film back into its space in the metal box, close the lid with a small clank. On the outside of the lid is a list of the reels stored inside. I scan the list, which I have not noticed before, since this is the first time I have been in complete charge of the movie projector. I notice that the last item on the list reads simply MERCER.

Mercer. Nana and Papa and Mom and Uncle Hayden and Adam. Not Owen. Not Dad and me.

I open the box again and find the reel labeled MERCER. I thread the film in the projector, turn out the light, and sit in the chair holding my breath. The image that flickers on the screen is old and grainy, but not as old and grainy as I had thought it might be.

A young woman in her cap and gown steps before the camera, holds up her diploma, smiles and waves. Mom. I remember the photo in the album, Mom graduating from high school. Is this the same graduation? Then Uncle Hayden appears behind her, dapper in his suit, and he looks so serious and grown up, so very much like Papa, that I know this must be Mom's college graduation. I smile. This is Mount Holyoke, then. This is South Hadley, Massachusetts, and the year must be 1943.

Adam would have been five then, I am thinking, and suddenly he bursts into the picture. He's wearing a suit and tie and the perfectly round glasses, and he runs to Mom and throws his arms around her waist. Mom takes off her cap and puts it on his head, and Adam turns to the camera and crosses his eyes and sticks out his tongue. Then he does a silly dance before he takes off the hat and hands it back to Mom.

I am smiling and tears are running down my cheeks and I don't think I can watch any more of the film. I don't know how to stop it in the middle, though, so I let it play out silently in the parlor while I sit in the kitchen.

I pick at what's left of the popcorn and think about the summer, the summer that was both awful and wonderful. I thank Adam, as I have thanked him almost every night since August, for showing me that it's possible to lift the corners of our universe. Adam told me about lifting the corners the second time I met him, but I had no idea what he meant. Now I think I do. It's all about changing what's handed to you, about poking around a little, lifting the corners, seeing what's underneath, poking that. Sometimes things work out, sometimes they don't, but at least you're exploring. And life is always more interesting that way.

Author's Note

Like Hattie in *A Corner of the Universe,* I found out as a young girl that I had had another uncle, and that he had been mentally ill. Unlike Hattie, however, I never had a chance to meet him. My uncle, Stephen, died in 1950, five years before I was born and about a year before my parents met each other. Some of the details in this book are real. I used them to make the story come alive. But I know very little about Stephen, and so the portrayal of Adam in this book is not based on Stephen. Adam is an imaginary character. And while Adam's family configuration — parents, older brother and sister — resembles Stephen's, Nana and Papa do not represent my loving grandparents, and Hattie's uncle and mother are not my uncle and mother. Nevertheless, Adam has had a great impact on me. He has given me the courage to lift the corners of my own universe. And I thank him for that.